I0618289

The Swamp Witches

Abigail Fero

CONTENTS

WELCOME TO THE SWAMP

Grandma stood at the threshold of her front door. Her white hair was bundled haphazardly on top of her head, pinned in place with several bone combs. The layers she wore hid her body and swathed her from head to toe in various neutral shades. Her mismatched eyes stared out at the vegetation that hedged her in. She waited.

They were only minutes away. The swamp knew their every move and she could feel their worries and fears and the little girl's confusion. She knew when they hesitated outside the clearing that surrounded her house. The overgrowth looked impenetrable but Grandma only allowed them to wait a moment before she reached out with her power and pulled the hedge back, just enough to show them which direction they needed to go.

She didn't even have to move. She could do everything from her front porch, the land so steeped in her presence that it forgot how to act without her direction. Visitors were rare but she knew that these ones were special; they came to give instead of take.

Their bobbing heads were the first things she saw. Both the mother and father had tangles of brown hair, struggling to hide pale, drawn faces. The little girl was the last, holding both her parents' hands, her eyes darting back and forth between them anxiously.

The mother looked relieved when she saw Grandma standing, waiting. The woman didn't hesitate but rushed the other two up the stairs to stop in front of the older woman. Grandma's mussed hair did nothing to hide her face and the burning eyes in it.

The girl squeaked when she saw the watery blue eye and its mismatched pair, a tiny, beetle-black eye. The skin around it was shiny, white and scarred. The pupil was indistinguishable from the iris and the small girl couldn't look away. Neither could the parents.

"Grandma..." the mother started, unsure what to say or how to finish. She glanced down at her child, frowning as if just realizing the girl was still with her.

Taking pity, Grandma interrupted her, saying, "Come inside."

The three visitors were glad to do so, crossing the threshold into the main room in the first house. Grandma's house was made of three buildings, shacks that leaned against each other, propping each other up. Two of the buildings were empty, waiting. Grandma lived in only one of the buildings where she had her bedroom, workshop and living room. Only her living room was open to visitors.

The house was decorated with bones and Grandma could see her visitors' minds working, trying to decide if they were human or not. Though few people celebrated a zombie kill by keeping a memento, it wasn't unheard of. As a witch of the swamp, there were certain expectations she was held to.

"Take a seat," Grandma said, ushering them closer to the fireplace. There were two wooden chairs and a stool. The girl took the stool without a thought and Grandma nodded her approval.

"Actually..." the mother started.

"Maybe it would be best if Maga played outside," the father finished.

Maga looked simultaneously delighted and terrified by the prospect. Children in the swamp did not play outside. It was hardly safe and though many of the children grew up knowing how to defend themselves, it was impossible to know of zombie swarms in advance.

"Don't worry," Grandma said to the child, "it's perfectly safe in the clearing. The heads can't get in."

Maga still didn't look reassured and Grandma couldn't blame her. The old woman had seen her own reflection and it wasn't a particularly comforting image. Only when both the mother and father nodded their blessing did the girl get up and go outside, though not without a few wary glances over her shoulder.

Grandma turned to the parents. She crossed her arms over her chest and waited. They both sighed and looked at each other. It was unusual to see a strong family unit in the swamp. Ties tended to be ephemeral, short-lived.

"How can I help?" Grandma asked.

"We've heard…" the father said.

"We've heard that you've been looking for a…a…" the mother tried to finish. "An apprentice."

The man and woman looked relieved to have gotten it out. Grandma sat down on the stool and leaned closer to the pair in front of her, a low-lying fire at her back. She'd kept it burning in anticipation of their visit.

"An apprentice, you say?" Grandma mused aloud. It was true, though apprentice wasn't quite the word she would have used. She was looking for someone special, someone with talent, someone with destiny.

"Yes, an apprentice," the father gushed, glad to have found what he was trying to say.

"And you think…?" Grandma asked, letting them fill in the blanks. She was having to do far more work than she'd anticipated in this conversation.

"We think Maga's the one for you," the girl's mother said. Her eyes were shining with sincerity and unshed tears.

"What makes you think that?"

"She…she talks to animals and she isn't like the other children in our camp-"

"Do the animals talk back?" Grandma cut the father off before he could ramble any more about how precious, different and *special* his little girl was.

"What?" The question confused both the parents and they looked at each other in bewilderment.

"Do they answer her when she talks to them?" Grandma asked again, patiently.

"No- I don't think…she's never…" the mother stumbled through an answer.

"Why?" the father asked.

"It's one thing for a child to talk to wild animals, it's quite something else for the animals to respond."

"Oh."

"Why do you want to give her to me?" Grandma asked, turning to the important question. Their answer might dictate whether or not she seriously considered the child.

"Give her-?"

"If she was to become my apprentice, she would live here with me. You wouldn't see her again. Once you left, she would forget all about you."

There was silence. The fire crackled, puffing a stream of smoke into the room. Grandma said nothing as she waited for a response.

"I ... thought about it," the mother broke the silence "I know we wouldn't be part of each other's lives anymore."

"So?" Grandma asked. That didn't answer her question. There was nothing in it for them. She offered no reward, no payment. It was difficult enough for children to be left by their parents, let alone to have been sold.

"It's not safe…out there," the father answered. "We aren't from here."

Few people *were* originally from the swamp. Most were immigrants, running for the safest place the world had to offer. The walking bodies were unable to penetrate the marshy land and while flying heads swarmed the swamp, they were preferable. Though they were deadly, the flying zombie heads were also stupid and one could survive with some quality of life if they adjusted to the swamp, and to killing, fast enough.

"She would be safe with you. She'd learn…how to be safe," the father ended lamely. His wife nodded and reached out to clutch his hand.

There was a squawk from outside. Grandma sat up. It wasn't just any bird and she left the parents sitting in their chairs. The door took little effort to open, despite not fitting its frame.

Grandma whistled sharply, her black eye searching the air in the clearing and the leaves hanging on the trees. Maga was nowhere to be found but the little girl wasn't who she sought. The bird sounded off again and Grandma followed the noise, trying to stay calm. She hadn't noticed until now the panic built up just under her diaphragm, coming from her familiar.

He was outside the clearing and the hedges stood aside for the old woman. She splashed through the water that filled the swamp, searching for the source of the noise and the panic. She cursed herself for being too distracted to notice. It was hard to distinguish between her panic and her familiar's panic as both grew. She shouldn't have sent the bird out with the girl.

Grandma whistled again and the answering voice echoed from close by. The old woman found them behind a clump of bushes. The gator gleamed dully in the dim light, its black hide blending into the water that concealed its lower body. Maga was crouched not too far away but Grandma couldn't see her familiar, the bird who made her witchery so much easier.

"Shhh," Maga said, not turning.

Grandma froze.

"He's in its mouth," Maga told the old woman.

The girl was right. The flutter of a nervous woodpecker was obvious behind the cage of the gator's teeth. It was holding the bird gently but the threat was evident. The woodpecker calmed slightly, sensing Grandma's presence but Grandma's heart still galloped.

Gators were the least reasonable of the animals and this one had a nasty glint in its eye. She knew it was young, too young to be sensible. Grandma and the gators respected each other and each other's space. This was far beyond the terms of any truce.

Grandma didn't know whether she was trembling from fear or fury. Neither boded well for the gator and she wasn't sure he'd go unpunished even if he let the woodpecker go. There were some games one didn't play.

Maga crawled closer and closer. The gator swung its head so it could watch her. The golden-brown eyes hooded.

"Woodpeckers aren't tasty," Maga was saying as she crept closer. "Yucky birds."

The gator snorted. It didn't believe a word she said. Grandma's mouth tightened. There was no way the gator didn't understand who was in his mouth. The woodpecker had finally stilled, though Grandma could feel its panic pulsating below the surface.

"Give me the bird," Maga said, her hand slowly reaching out.

The gator waggled its head back and forth. It wasn't willing to give up such a prize.

"You don't want him, he's dirty. Besides, you're upsetting Grandma," Maga said softly.

Grandma stared at the back of the six-year-old's head. The tangled mess of curls created a halo around her. She missed the inspection the gator gave her.

"You don't want to upset Grandma, do you?" Maga asked.

"She looks pretty scary."

The gator looked over at the old woman again, considering her carefully. Grandma scowled at it, her black eye sparkling fiercely. She didn't say a word, wanting to see how Maga would handle the situation. As she gained control of her emotions, Grandma's fear left her. The gator was young and it didn't know her. It didn't know what she could do; what she would do.

"Give me the birdy," Maga said, her voice tilting, caressing the words until they sounded like a song.

The gator hesitated but the teeth pulled apart minutely. The woodpecker's beak appeared in the gap between two teeth, frantically pecking, drilling for freedom.

"Hush," Grandma soothed the bird. It was all under control now and there was no need to aggravate the situation. Besides, as a familiar, he was afforded certain protections, though there had never been need before to see how far those could stretch.

Grandma's voice snapped the gator back to attention and it growled at her. She snarled back, frightening the child stuck between them.

"Maga, go back inside," Grandma said, not even looking at the girl.

Maga scrambled backwards, making tracks through the mud. Grandma could hear her splashing through the water and struggling through the hedges around the clearing. She waited until she couldn't hear the girl any longer before she turned to the gator.

"Now you may be young enough and *stupid* enough to think you can get away with this," Grandma hissed, "but the truce we have protects *you*, not me."

The old woman sprung at the gator, her teeth bared. It startled backwards in surprise, its teeth gaping. She grabbed tight to the jaws and bent, prying them open, surprising the monster with her strength. The gator snuffled and snorted, trying to shake her off but it wasn't long before the jaws were wide enough that the woodpecker jumped out.

Once the bird was free, Grandma let the jaws snap back together. The gator shook its head, dazed. The woodpecker trilled from behind Grandma, fluffing its feathers until it resembled a bird again.

"Now, you might want to go home, because you can be sure,

I'll be back," Grandma growled before turning her back on the beast, stomping back to the clearing.

The bushes snapped away from her, letting her pass without brushing a single leaf. The woodpecker followed behind quietly. She could feel his embarrassment.

Bypassing the worried parents standing on the porch, Grandma marched straight up to Maga, grabbing the little girl's arm.

"And just what do you think you were doing?" Grandma asked.

"I was trying to help your birdy," Maga said.

"Don't you know that gators eat little girls?" Grandma asked, thrusting her face into Maga's. The girl barely flinched.

"It wasn't going to hurt me. It was just being mean."

Grandma released Maga, straightening up to meet the parents' eyes. They gulped, looking as worried as they should be.

"I'll take her," Grandma said abruptly before turning on her heel and stalking off to her workshop.

Their surprise radiated at her back but she didn't want to deal with them anymore. She left the family to say their goodbyes and the parents to make their explanations. Grandma wasn't sure how much Maga knew about why she was here.

"And what do you think *you* were doing?" Grandma asked the woodpecker once they were in the privacy of her workroom. The bird cheeped, hanging its head in shame. His single eye blinked at her in remorse.

"You're lucky," Grandma ended up saying.

The bird agreed with her and Grandma felt her fury disappear. She stroked the bird's head, relieved her familiar was unharmed.

"I think we must make a visit tonight," Grandma said, exhaling. The bird rubbed its beak along her finger, chirping.

"Yes, I know very well that you'll be coming with me," the old woman said. "This is just what I need, trouble with the gators. And on top of the girl as well."

Despite her words, Grandma was hardly upset at having to make the visit. After Maga's performance, Grandma was intrigued and she had a new leverage against the gators. They'd be partial to the girl and repentant over their youngster's rash behavior.

Grandma left not long after sundown, letting Maga's parents stay the night so that she could make this visit. With her familiar perched on her shoulder, his feet dug into the fabric on her shoulder, Grandma made the journey.

The gators had a gathering pool not too far from the clearing where Grandma lived so it wasn't too long a trip. They were waiting for her when she arrived, their eyes gleaming from the inky water. She wasn't afraid and she waited, somewhat impatiently.

"Well?" Grandma finally asked.

There was a rumble and a set of yellow eyes rose up to become the largest gator. It slowly rolled up to the island of firm land that Grandma was standing on, her familiar perched on her shoulder. Grandma refused to stoop down to meet the animal eye-to-eye. She wasn't amused and she wasn't willing to make any concessions.

"One of yours was on my land today. I demand reparations," Grandma told him.

The woodpecker fluffed itself angrily on her shoulder, hooting derisively at the gator. It was only the beginning of the negotiations, something that could last as long or as short as the gators were willing to make it. This time, she knew it shouldn't take long. They needed to placate her and that wouldn't be done by drawing this meeting out.

The meeting didn't last long and they came to a tentative agreement. The verbal contract between them had to be changed though they differed on the changes to be made.

Grandma spent the rest of the night in her workshop, unwilling to leave until she had a first draft drawn up. She worked better when she had the contract written down. Though the gators' memory was strong enough to hold the entire contract, Grandma wanted proof of what they'd agree on. She wanted something to stare at and niggle with.

The woodpecker watched her with his single black eye, only warning her when the sun started to rise. She looked up from the bark she'd been scrawling on, brushed a hand wearily over her eyes and got to her feet.

"I guess I need to speak to the family," Grandma sighed. The woodpecker agreed and flew over to her shoulder, settling down quickly.

The family waited in the living room, awake and anxious. Maga's father clutched the girl close and all three faces were pale and drawn.

"Maga…" Grandma said, trying to find the words. Her head was fuzzy after a long night and she didn't want to say the wrong thing. It had been a long time since she'd had a family and a long time since she'd felt vulnerable.

"She knows why we're here," the father cut in. Grandma shot him a look but he nodded and so did the girl's mother.

"I'll be safe here," Maga said, unsure.

"You will be safe here," Grandma agreed.

"And there's not enough space for three?" Maga asked.

"We're giving you a future. Grandma is giving you a future," Maga's mother said, reaching out to touch her cheek. "Your father and I already had our future, it's your turn."

Grandma walked Maga's mother and father to the hedge. The girl's goodbye had been tearful and she'd locked herself away in the room Grandma set up for her, a small space in one of the empty buildings. Her parents were barely keeping it together though there was a clear gratitude shining through.

"Why?" Maga's mother asked as Grandma pulled back the foliage to let them pass.

"I'm not sure yet," Grandma said. "But I don't think any of us will regret it." She wouldn't give the woman empty platitudes so she hoped her simple words would be enough comfort.

"Thanks," the father said. "We're struggling here in the swamp. It's only a matter of time before…"

He didn't have to finish his sentence. Grandma knew what he meant. Sometimes it was difficult for people to adjust and those were the ones that didn't last.

It wasn't her job to help everyone. She was part of something larger than the individual lives of humanity. She didn't have much to do with the individuals. Grandma looked at the bigger picture. Maga's parents weren't part of that and yet she couldn't just let them go.

The woodpecker squawked when Grandma reached and plucked two feathers from the bird. With the sharp edge of the quill, Grandma stabbed her arm, soaking the feathers in her blood. The parents watched on, horrified as she waved them in the air, drying and dyeing the feathers.

Grandma handed the two feathers over to the parents. They reluctantly took the bloodied feathers, staring at her in confusion.

"If you take these to the citadel and give them to the Seer, they'll let you stay. You'll be safe there."

"Why are you doing this?"

"Maga needs to know you'll be safe and I've never been a very good liar," Grandma said with a shrug. A hank of white hair fell across her blue eye and she watched them with her black, woodpecker eye as they turned and left.

Maga watched the old woman out of the smudged window. Her parents were each clutching a feather as Grandma talked to them. Maga knew they were leaving but the raw hope on their faces told her something had changed for them. Grandma changed something for them.

The room Maga stood in was small and the bed was rough. There was only one blanket and nothing else in the space but dirty wooden floorboards. Maga didn't want her parents to go and her eyes were red and puffy from crying.

She didn't know Grandma and she'd never been away from her mom and dad. It was scary and nothing about this place seemed safe to her. There were bones everywhere and the old woman's eyes were creepy. She didn't want to stay but she had no choice. She had to be brave just like her mom said.

It was going to be tough, but life in the swamp was hard. Sometimes, at camp, the oldest people told stories about life before the zombies. About life outside the swamp. Maga wasn't sure they were even telling the truth but it sounded wonderful all the same. She wished she could live outside the swamp. Instead she was here with Grandma and she knew there was something they weren't telling her.

The old woman returned to the house but Maga wasn't watching her. She kept her eyes on her parents until she couldn't see them any longer. Even when the swamp foliage swallowed them entirely, she couldn't take her eyes away. She was lucky, she knew. Most kids didn't have any parents, let alone two. But here she was, watching hers walk away.

Grandma came with dinner but Maga paid her no mind. She didn't want to talk and she didn't want to see the old woman.

"Eat your dinner," Grandma said as she laid the bowl of soup down.

"I don't wanna," Maga mumbled, still watching out the window.

"Eat one bite and then I'll leave."

Maga looked over at the old woman and saw that she wouldn't be moved. She turned from the window and grabbed the spoon lying in the bowl. One sip. The flavor of the broth exploded over her tongue, making her eyes water. Grandma nodded in satisfaction and handed her a rough piece of bread. Maga tore into it, trying to soothe her mouth.

"Let me see your eyes," Grandma said after Maga swallowed.

The girl looked up at the old woman reluctantly. Something about Grandma's mismatched eyes was creepy. The washed out blue eye was normal enough but the black, woodpecker eye burned. She couldn't look away.

"How do you feel?" Grandma asked, her voice sounding very far away.

"I feel fine," Maga responded, her mind curiously blank as the words rose from somewhere. She didn't know where they came from but when she said them, they sounded profoundly true and right.

"Good."

Grandma turned and left, leaving the soup and the rest of the bread there for Maga. Shaking her head, Maga scowled at the bowl of soup. It looked suspicious. But hunger eventually won out and she took a cautious sip. Frowning, she swallowed and took another. It was good, better than she'd had in a while, but there was nothing strange about it.

No one came to take the empty bowl and plate away. After a while, Maga went back to watching the window, more out of boredom than anything else. She vaguely remembered she was looking for something before but now she couldn't recall what it was.

When night fell, something finally crossed in front of the window. Grandma, wrapped up in numerous scarves and shawls ambled out across the clearing. The hedges danced aside for her and swallowed her shadow up. Maga perked up considerably. Something was going on. She was curious.

Maga tried sneaking after Grandma but lost her twice before finding her again. She didn't want to get caught but she was curious. Left alone in the house in the middle of the night, she had to know what Grandma was up to. It was better than lying down in the scratchy bed alone in the room.

She was good at skulking and she moved pretty silently

through the swamp. Grandma was fixated on something, her thoughts far away. Even the woodpecker didn't notice the little girl.

They eventually stopped though it was too dark to see where they were. Maga hid behind a tree as Grandma stood on the edge of a black pool of water. She gasped quietly when the gators rose out of the pool.

"So, I've looked things over," Grandma said, a piece of bark clutched in one hand. 'I think the terms are fair, especially after that close call we had.'

One of the alligators growled, a low rumble erupting from its long face. Grandma chuckled.

"You should have thought of that before you let your ignorant youngsters wander. You're lucky familiars aren't as fragile as they look. But if anything were to happen to him, or the girl, the terms are null and void."

The alligator responded with a snarl.

"It shouldn't matter who she is," Grandma snapped. "She's off limits."

Maga wondered if they were talking about her. They had to be but she didn't understand. Her feet shifted in the mud, sending her tilting back away from the tree. She scrambled to right herself and when she looked up, Grandma's woodpecker stared at her with his one black eye. Maga whimpered.

He jumped from the tree to her shoulder. The claws bit into her skin through the thin fabric and she knew she was caught. The bird trilled in her ear, pushing her along. Maga turned her back reluctantly on the scene between Grandma and the gators. The woodpecker sat, a heavy burden, weighing her shoulder down until they made it back to the clearing. The bird stayed with her until she entered her room. Once she sat down on her bed, the bird left her.

It was hard to fall asleep that night. Maga lay awake in the bed until the early hours of the morning. She dozed off eventually and when she woke, she was still tired. Sitting up, her head pounded and her mouth felt fuzzy. Last night was clear and sharp in her memory but something was missing before that. She couldn't remember the last week very clearly and when she tried to concentrate on it, her memory slipped from her grasp. She gave up and went to find food.

Grandma waited in the kitchen, with a chair pulled back in invitation, hot food on the table. Maga sat down hesitantly, looking up at the old woman through her eyelashes. The woodpecker would have told on her.

"Look at me," Grandma said, leaning over the table, her two eyes gleaming. "What do you remember of last month?"

Maga scrunched her face, staring at the old woman. She didn't understand the question. She tried to keep her eyes on Grandma's as she thought about last month.

"Well?" Grandma asked impatiently

"You can be precocious, just make sure you aren't stupid," Grandma said casually.

Maga nodded hesitantly when the old woman fixed her with a stare. She didn't ask what precocious meant.

"Good," Grandma said, satisfied with that.

"That's it?" Maga asked, stupefied that there wasn't more trouble waiting for her.

"That's it, girl. You won't be getting lectures on how to live your life from the likes of me. I would just prefer you stay alive for the time being." Grandma leaned over the table and whispered, "we aren't done with you." She finished with a wink and Maga had a feeling the woodpecker was grinning.

Swamp Familiars

There was a boy in the forest. Maga first saw him days ago, a brief glimpse deep in the swamp foliage, a flash of black hair through green leaves. At first she thought he was just someone passing through, it wasn't completely unheard of.

Just because Grandma rarely had any visitors and people tended to steer clear of her land, didn't mean the occasional person didn't make an appearance. The swamp was full of travelers and camps of people, Maga just didn't see many of them. Once she'd lived among them, though her memory of those days was foggy, but now they were an irregularity. She certainly never saw anyone more than once.

But he didn't just make one appearance. She spotted the boy's curly black hair and blue eyes everywhere she went. It was as if he was following her, though Maga knew he hadn't spotted her yet. She had a talent for camouflage.

The boy was everywhere, most often in her thoughts. Maga's previous hobbies, which included spying on Grandma, foraging or stalking any animal she could find, dwindled. Her thoughts and time were now devoted to the walking anomaly.

She didn't think he knew about Grandma, which would explain why he was intent on settling in the area. No one lived within at least a four mile radius of Grandma. Maga didn't know whether it was the old woman's doing or something about the area that kept people away.

For the first couple days, Maga kept the delicious secret to herself, sure that as soon as Grandma knew she'd scare the boy off somehow. It couldn't be a coincidence that no one lived near them. She spent less time watching Grandma and more time watching the boy. Locating him each morning was always a game tinged with the fear that she wouldn't find him- that he would be gone.

Eventually, when not a day went by without her spotting him, she felt comfortable that he wasn't going anywhere. She also knew that it was only a matter of time before he spotted her or stumbled through the thick foliage which hid Grandma's house and kept it safe. It was only a matter of time before she solved the mystery of the boy. Maga didn't want it to end but she didn't want him to be sent away either. It was time she told Grandma.

"There's a boy in the swamp."

Grandma spent most of her days tucked away in her workroom. Maga knew better than to penetrate any further than the threshold without express permission. As an eight year old, it was difficult for her to obey such strictures but Grandma's familiar policed the room and even her sneaking abilities couldn't help her with him.

"I know."

Maga frowned at Grandma's answer. The old woman only occasionally left the clearing and not at all since Maga had first seen the boy.

"How do you know?" Maga asked, her words addressed to Grandma's back.

The old woman turned to stare at her, the white hair swept away from her face with undecorated bone combs.

"I can see," Grandma said, her mismatched eyes boring holes into Maga's brown ones.

The little girl shivered. She'd only been living with Grandma just over two years now, though she couldn't quite remember how she lived before. The sight of Grandma's eyes still unnerved her and Maga couldn't help but stare. Grandma's normal blue eye was a bit faded and grey but it was the other one that gave Maga nightmares. Small, black and surrounded by puckered flesh, the tiny eye was impossible to look away from. It matched the single eye of Grandma's woodpecker.

Maga stood there a moment longer to see if that was all

Grandma had to say. Grandma's one-eyed bird stood on its perch and stared at Maga. When the old woman didn't speak again, Maga gave up waiting and headed for the door. It seemed as if her caretaker wasn't going to interfere.

That day, after her short conversation with Grandma, she found the boy perched on an island of firm ground not too far from the clearing. Maga was covered in swamp ooze, mud dripping down her face. She didn't want him to see her; she still hadn't decided when or how to introduce herself.

The boy didn't look prepared for the swamp. While the swamp was the least dangerous place left, with only an infestation of the stupidest zombies, it was far from safe. The boy didn't have a blindfold, a necessary item to have at least hanging around the neck. The flying heads' ability to mesmerize its prey was most of what made the stupid things so dangerous. But the boy had no blindfold or weapon. He didn't even have a bag. She wondered how he was surviving out here without food, surely he had to be eating something.

Normally an anxious and fidgety girl, Maga was experiencing a patience she'd never had before. Grandma despaired of her attention span, unable to get her to sit still long enough to learn anything. Maga knew the time would come when she could but she just wasn't ready yet. There was still so much playing and exploring to do.

Through the muck, an ominous hum filled Maga's ears and her brown eyes widened, watching the boy to see what he would do. When he continued to sit there, staring into space, Maga started to get worried. The hum was getting louder and the boy only just noticed. He twisted around, trying to see where the noise was coming from.

Maga launched herself out of the mud. She tackled the boy to the ground and wrestled him into the swamp. He was stronger and bigger than she was but Maga was desperate to keep them both hidden. She hadn't brought a weapon, it had been a long time since she'd needed one. The heads usually stayed away from Grandma's place.

"Get down!" Maga growled at the boy.

He got away from her but looked up in time to see the flickering of the flying heads through the trees. He gasped and he dove down beside her. Maga scooped mud onto his head and pushed him deeper into the water. They closed their eyes, squeezing them tightly, hoping they wouldn't be noticed.

The humming hovered by the island they'd just tumbled off of and Maga held her breath. Maga slit one of her eyes open, looking through her eyelashes to watch. If they had to fight, she wanted some warning. Their empty, scarred eye sockets held no eyes but that never slowed them down and their pinched, withered nostrils looked useless but they could ferret out a hiding human with worrying precision. No one really knew how the flying heads worked, not even Grandma.

The boy trembled next to her, their hands tightly clasped together. She felt a whimper building up in his throat and she crushed his hand, hoping to keep him silent. The heads bobbed above the swamp floor for a second or two longer before disappearing. Maga didn't immediately get up and didn't let the boy rise either. They stayed in the cool, slick slime until Maga was sure the heads weren't coming back.

"It's ok, they're gone," Maga said, pulling the boy up with her.

He was even bigger now that she had time to look at him. He towered over her though he didn't look much older. He looked down at her, his eyes standing out from the muddy face.

"What were you doing?" Maga asked when the silence got too much for her. "Don't you know anything?"

"I was just sitting," the boy mumbled.

"Didn't you hear them?"

"I didn't know what it was."

"*Everyone* knows that sound," Maga said, suspicious. "Just how long have you been here?"

The boy shrugged and didn't reply. When it was obvious he had nothing else to say and no real explanation for his stupidity, Maga huffed and grabbed his hand.

"We should go get cleaned up," she told him. She didn't think Grandma would mind having the boy in the house.

The boy followed her sedately back through the foliage which protected the clearing. He looked unsure as they approached but when Maga wriggled through a hole in the hedge, he followed without a word.

Once they'd cleaned up and the boy's damp hair was starting to spring back into its curls, Maga found some food for him.

"Thanks," he said, snatching the rice cake from her hand.

She grinned, hopping up onto the other rough chair at the table. The wooden seats were worn smooth in places but the danger of splinters was always present. Neither Grandma nor Maga was good with wood.

They sat and stared at each other. Maga replaced the rice cake five more times before he slowed.

"I'm Maga," she said, her elbows propped up on the table, her chin resting in her palms. She couldn't stop staring, entranced by his presence.

"Doxin," the boy said, looking at her, his expression torn between wariness and awe.

"You don't belong in the swamp," Maga told him.

He didn't reply but continued to sit there and watch her. After a while Maga couldn't take the silence any longer. There was too much silence in the clearing.

"Wanna go play?" Maga asked.

The boy nodded hesitantly but got to his feet once Maga was on hers. She led the way back out through the clearing into the swamp. She only knew how to play by herself so they did what she enjoyed doing. They climbed trees, stalked animals and swam through the swamp. Doxin was never far behind her and while he didn't smile, his eyes were lit with pleasure.

The end of the day came quicker than she thought it would and they were dangling from a tree when she noticed how dark it was getting. She didn't know where Doxin spent his nights but he survived this long and she wasn't sure he'd be welcome at Grandma's.

"Sunset! I better get going. See you tomorrow, Doxin!" Maga said, hopping down out of the tree they'd been swinging in.

She waved when she got to the ground and disappeared into the hedge. Maga could feel him watching her from the top of the tree.

Maga climbed into her bed, unable to stop smiling. Grandma came in, as she always did to say goodnight, stooping to blow out the tallow candle. The moon shone in through the window, lighting up the floor.

"I had the best day ever, Grandma," Maga said as the old woman pulled up the blankets gathered around Maga's feet. "Do you think he'll stay?"

"It depends," Grandma answered.

"On what?"

"Was he a nice boy?" Grandma asked.

Her voice was rougher than usual and Maga wondered if she'd spoken all day. She was used to Grandma's roundabout way of talking and seeming inability to answer the questions asked.

"I don't know. But his name is Doxin and we're going to play again tomorrow." Maga snuggled down into the blankets, smiling beatifically up at the ceiling.

"Are you ready?" Grandma asked, wiping the smile from Maga's face.

Maga didn't reply, only turned over in the bed, presenting Grandma with her back. Maga tucked her hands up under her cheek and scowled at the wooden wall. Grandma stood there for a heartbeat before leaving the room.

Maga didn't know how many times she'd been asked that since she first arrived two years ago. Grandma never explained what she meant and past conversations revealed that she wouldn't. It was supposed to be something Maga figured out on her own. After two years of the same question, it never failed to irritate her and make her angry, though she couldn't quite explain why.

When Maga woke in the morning, the scowl was still scrawled across her face. Grandma was at the table and Maga wasn't sure if it was because the old woman had woken up late or that she, herself, had woken up early.

Breakfast was silent and Maga could feel Grandma's gaze on her face. She never raised her eyes to meet the mismatched ones across from her. Maga planned on eating quickly and storming out of the house but the old woman beat her to it and disappeared into her workroom. Maga could hear the squawk of the woman's familiar and the frown deepened.

Maga finished her food quickly, some of it getting stuck in her throat. She washed it down with nettle tea Grandma left on the table. Growling, the little girl entered the clearing, still inexplicably angry about last night.

"He better still be here," Maga muttered to herself.

Doxin was right where she'd left him. They stared at each other, one in the tree and one on the ground. Maga's foul mood wasn't any better and she glared at the boy. He scowled back, the expression made for his face.

"Well, are you coming down or not?" Maga snapped.

Doxin stood for a moment, his feet precariously balanced on a limb, before he slipped down through the tree to land in front of the girl. Her scowl didn't lessen and neither did his. They stood, arms crossed against their chests, glaring at each other.

Maga didn't know how to handle Doxin frowning at her. Grandma never had moods and tolerated Maga's with a patience Maga didn't share.

"What are you so angry about?" Maga snapped.

"Dunno, what are *you* so angry about?" Doxin replied.

His questions brought her up short.

"I don't know," she said slowly, testing the answer in her mouth.

She stood there, wondering about her mood. It suddenly dissipated as the two of them stood there. Examined in the light of day, she had no reason to be mad at Grandma. She didn't know what she was supposed to be ready for but someday she would and until then, it wasn't something she had to worry about.

Doxin stared at her curiously as she stood silent, thinking. When he saw her face lighten, his own scowl fell from his face. He waited.

"I'm not angry anymore," Maga said eventually.

"Good," Doxin replied.

"Wanna see something cool?"

"Okay."

"Let's go, then," Maga crowed before diving into the swamp.

She rarely wore the clunky boots others found necessary as she rarely went far and her slight shoes provided all the protection she needed. Maga didn't want the heavy boots weighing her down, though she did own a pair. Doxin was similarly clad and neither of them had any difficulty sloshing through the swamp waters.

Maga was thrilled to lead the way, delighted to have someone to share her secrets with. Doxin followed behind her without any questions and she led him further and further from the clearing where she lived. Maga knew exactly where she was going.

She froze on the edge of the water, her destination spread out in front of her. Cradled in the swamp was a dark pool that held the objects of all her fascination. Until Doxin came along, Maga spent many of her days perched in the trees, watching. She flung up a hand when Doxin tripped over a root, making too much noise. Doxin paused in the act of climbing to his feet, his breath stuttering behind her. He'd finally seen them.

Bright yellow eyes blinked into existence, their slit pupils staring at the pair of children. Maga held her breath, her palms sweating and her face flushing. They were magnificent as they rose up from the depths of the pool, their black flesh peeling back the surface of the water, their nostrils flaring.

"Gators," Doxin breathed as he stared, spellbound.

Maga grinned. "Gators," she agreed.

Since she'd seen them with Grandma two years ago, arguing about something, she'd become fixated.

Doxin didn't seem as pleased as she was, grabbing her arm and pulling her down into the mud, dragging her away from the pool. The alligators rose, their interest piqued by Maga's scream. Doxin rolled, his body covering Maga's. Their heartbeats pattered against one another. Neither of them spoke as the first gator touched the mud inches from their frightened faces.

Maga had watched the creatures, but she'd never gotten this close before. Her face was frozen in a rictus of fear and fascination. Of all the animals she'd ever seen, the gator was her favorite and she longed for the day she might understand them the way Grandma did.

Maga found herself shuffled further under Doxin's body until her face was hidden against his chest. She knew Doxin was staring into the golden eyes. The gators growing ever closer, she could feel his heart pounding. At least he knew not to move or look away as two more gators reached the mud embankment. Sweat dripped from his face to land on Maga's arm. It burned but neither of them moved. Finally she rolled so she could see what was happening.

The first gator opened its mouth, the wide grimace revealing jagged teeth and fetid breath. Maga tried not to choke at the salty smell of decaying flesh. Doxin, frozen above her, didn't seem able to look away from the alligator. It crept closer and closer until the edge of its snout was only a fingerbreadth away from Doxin's nose.

The ground trembled under the belly of the beast and a growl erupted from its widespread mouth. Doxin couldn't keep the whimper in his throat and the gator snuffled in response. It was laughing at him, Maga could tell.

She could hear everything that was going on. They were being toyed with and she wasn't happy. Her irritation rose up against the fear. Her eyebrows snapped together and she could feel the scowl forming itself. She scooted further out from under Doxin, rolling until her head rested under his chin.

Maga glared at the gator and its eyes left Doxin's to meet hers. She could see surprise in the yellow depths and that did nothing to calm her. She snorted at the gator and it reared back. Doxin's heart picked up speed and he leaned heavily on Maga. She fought back and snorted at the gator again.

Then she opened her mouth and bellowed at it, her frustration and anger tingeing her tone. The gator froze for a moment before snuffling once again. Soon all the gators were chortling, their laughter bubbling up through the water.

The three who had emerged from the water shuffled back down into it, their eyes never leaving Maga's until they were covered in the black water. The yellow, golden and brown eyes winked out as they disappeared again until there was just the one set staring. The gator winked and then closed its eyes and sunk until only its nostrils were visible.

Doxin broke form first, scrambling backwards away from the water, pulling Maga with him. She let him drag her through the swamp and whenever one of them tripped, the other hauled them up and hurried them along. As they broke back into familiar ground, she stopped and leaned against a tree, holding her sides and panting.

Doxin looked at Maga, her hair tangled in a halo around her face, strands dripping down over her shoulders. Maga stared back before breaking out into laughter. Doxin watched for a moment before joining in. They rolled against the tree, the nervous laughter getting louder and louder. Every time it looked like they might stop, they caught each other's eye and started all over again.

"I can't believe you," Doxin panted in between breaths.

"Me either!" Maga agreed.

When the laughter finally ran its course, the two children were relieved and elated in turns. Instead of staying outside, Maga made a quick decision and grabbed Doxin's arm. He let her drag him through the swamp, following as closely as she'd allow. They pierced the hedge surrounding the witch's clearing and Maga bounded up to the workroom she knew Grandma would be in.

The door flew open under Maga's enthusiasm but Grandma didn't turn away from her roughly hewn table. The woodpecker turned its head, cocking it at an impossible angle, fixing them with its one, beady, black eye. It trilled and Grandma finally looked up from whatever she was holding. Her back straightened and they stood on the threshold, both frozen in anticipation. Doxin wiped a sweaty hand on his dirty shorts, smearing mud. Maga reached out and grabbed his hand, not wanting him to make a bigger mess.

"Grandma?"

"Hello, boy," Grandma said, ignoring Maga. Her attention was fixed on the ragged, muddy boy.

"Hi," Doxin replied, his voice barely audible.

The old woman turned to better study them. A hank of white hair had fallen over her face, covering the black eye. She reached a wrinkled hand up to put it back in place. Doxin gasped when he saw what the hair hid. Grandma grinned at him. All her teeth were in place, white and incongruent in the withered face.

"So, you found him, did you?" Grandma asked Maga.

Maga's brow wrinkled. She wasn't sure what Grandma meant. The woman spoke in riddles and Maga was still learning all the layers.

"I told you there was a boy in the swamp," Maga reminded the woman. "Can I keep him?"

Grandma looked at Doxin, shuffling closer to see him better. She squinted, grabbing his face and holding it up to the light. The woodpecker hopped over to look as well. Their black eyes matched and Maga tried to keep her shudder at bay.

"You've chosen well," Grandma said. "Unusual, though."

"Is that a yes?" Maga just wanted to know if he could stay. She hadn't even bothered asking Doxin but she knew he'd want to stay with her. She couldn't say how she knew but there was a connection between the two of them, tenuous but clearly there.

"How about we have some lunch and you two tell me where you've been," Grandma said, a hand on each of their shoulders as she spun the children away from her, marching them next door.

Once they were all seated, Doxin on a small stool, Grandma repeated her question as the kids dove into their soup, a lumpy piece of bread clutched in each hand.

"Well, Doxin and I went exploring," Maga started. "I thought

I'd show him the gators." Maga went through the events, talking faster and faster until she reached the climax of the story. "And then I bellowed at him and he went away! Doxin was shaking like a leaf, but I wasn't afraid," Maga bragged.

Doxin rolled his eyes but let her finish the story. Grandma sat there silently, her spoon suspended above the bowl. Her eyes flicked between the two of them, though the bird stared fixedly at Doxin.

"You ok with staying, boy?" Grandma asked Doxin.

He nodded as he chewed on the bread, hunger overtaking any manners he might have had. Maga still wasn't sure where his family was or how he'd survived so long in the swamp but at least if he stayed, he'd be safe and with a family of sorts.

"Well, not what I expected for your familiar but not a bad choice overall," Grandma told Maga.

"My familiar?"

Grandma had a familiar but she was a witch. Maga was just a little girl.

"Are you ready?" the old woman asked, ignoring Maga's question.

The old woman had never asked during the day before, always at night, just as Maga was about to go to sleep. Something had changed and looking over at Doxin, Maga thought it might have something to do with him.

Maga furrowed her brow, not snapping as she usually did when Grandma asked. This time it was different though she couldn't say how.

"I…" Maga started, unsure how to finish. Her gaze flicked over to Doxin's face again. He wasn't paying any attention to her and Grandma. Soup dripped down his chin but he didn't seem to mind, bent over the bowl as he was.

"I…I think I am," Maga said, the sentence sounding caught between a question and a revelation. She wasn't quite sure what she was agreeing to but it felt right, she felt ready for whatever lay ahead of her.

"Good. Then the two of you should go play because we start tomorrow," Grandma said, dropping her spoon and getting to her feet. "That goes for both of you," Grandma pointed a finger at Doxin and he froze mid-bite. He nodded and she smiled toothily at him before leaving them alone in the room.

"Come on, Doxin, eat faster!" Maga urged him, feeling light and unburdened.

Something had happened, something had changed but she didn't want to examine it, she wanted to be playing outside with her new friend.

Doxin slopped through the bowl, stuffing the last of the bread into his mouth.

"What starts tomorrow?" he asked, his mouth full.

Maga's smile vanished and she looked as puzzled as he felt. "I'm not sure…something important though."

Alone in the Swamp

Maga woke, disorientated. Her bedroom felt empty and she looked over to where Doxin slept. The bed was unrumpled and unslept in.

She groaned as she pulled back the blanket on her bed, grimacing when her feet touched the cold wooden boards. The swamp never got too chilly but after living there so long, her body became used to the warmer temperatures.

The house she lived in with her familiar, Doxin, echoed its emptiness. She knew that next door, where Grandma lived in her own leaning house, it would be similar. She forgot that Grandma and Doxin left last night. At twelve years old, she was, for the first time, all by herself.

Alone for two days, Maga wasn't quite sure she could cope. She'd never been alone before, certainly not for two whole days. Stepping out of the front door, onto the porch all three buildings shared, Maga turned right, heading for Grandma's house.

The first room was the dining room and living room combined. There was some bread left out on the table, a plate of greens next to it and a dried piece of fish. Maga sat down to the breakfast, glad she wouldn't have to scrounge something up for herself.

Next to the plate sat a scribbled list of chores for Maga. On a normal day she might have felt a twinge of irritation but today she was glad for the structure it would provide. Even Grandma's bird was gone. The wooden buildings creaked and she could hear the wind blowing through the leaves outside but there was no other sound. It was unusual.

She tried not to mind but once she'd eaten and cleaned her plate, the silence of the buildings drove her outside, her list clutched in one hand. On it Grandma laid out in detail just what she wanted done so that Maga couldn't say she misunderstood as she'd done before. But Maga had no intention of leaving the list unfulfilled. She didn't want Grandma leaving and taking Doxin with her ever again. It felt too much like a punishment.

"Fish, fish, fish," Maga sang to herself as she left the clearing behind, the list safely tucked away in one of her many pockets.

Out in the swamp she could almost believe that they were waiting for her back in the house. It made the day easier to bear but when the sun began to set and most of the chores on the list were completed, Maga had to drag herself back to the clearing.

Despite all her hard work, harder than normal as she tried to distract herself form the emptiness and loneliness, Maga wasn't hungry. She ate some of the flat cakes Grandma kept stored and went to bed. She knew that the sooner she went to sleep, the sooner the night would be over but she sat up in her bed, unable to close her eyes and fall asleep.

There was a quality to the darkness in her room. It wasn't the soft warmth and familiar shadows, it was something more sinister. The air felt dense and Maga had to stare hard at every shape before she could say, for sure, that it belonged in the room. She didn't have much hope for sleep in this new, hostile environment.

Hours after the sun had set she began hearing the noises. Something was inside the clearing. Nothing came inside except for the occasional animal or a supplicant, come to beg the swamp witch for whatever they needed. Maga grabbed her small knife that sat on the table next to her bed. Kicking the covers away, she didn't want anything to hold her back in case she needed to defend herself.

Even though she and Doxin both owned weapons, she didn't know very much about how to use one. She knew that many children in the swamp grew up fighting, killing and surviving on those abilities alone but since Grandma didn't use weapons, Maga had no one to learn from. When she'd asked to learn, Grandma refused.

"You want to be a swamp witch, don't you?" the old woman asked.

Maga nodded, unsure what that had to do with wanting to be able to defend herself.

"Swamp witches don't use weapons."

"But I'm not a swamp witch yet."

"That's true. I guess you'll just have to stay alive until you are."

That was the last Maga heard about it. Doxin thought Grandma's stance on the whole thing was ridiculous and Maga couldn't disagree. But she'd never really had need for the knife she carried, aside from gutting fish or harvesting plants. Once or twice she'd run into a flying head, one of the few human predators in the swamp, but it was a rare occurrence. She never really had anything to fear.

But without Grandma in the house, Maga felt very fearful. She heard the slosh of footsteps and a splash, a muttered curse. Sliding off her bed, Maga crept towards the door. She peeled it open as far as she could without it squeaking. The moonlight was dim in the clearing but it was still enough to illuminate the figure sneaking through.

"Doxin! What are you doing here?" Maga cried, throwing open the door when she recognized her familiar.

He grinned up at her from a face full of mud, on the outer edges of the clearing. "These hedges are getting worse. I could have sworn they didn't want to let me in."

Maga laughed, relief making her giddy. "I was so scared; I didn't know *what* you were."

"So it was you keeping me out. Did you think I was a zombie, come to eat your face?" he asked, springing to his feet and advancing towards her, gnashing his teeth.

"Stop it!" Maga said, batting him away from her as he approached. "You're filthy."

"Nom, nom, nom."

"Doxin, get away."

Maga half-heartedly pushed him away. She couldn't stop grinning, relieved beyond measure to see him, even if he scared her half to death. He finally relented and they went inside to clean him up and get to bed.

"Why are you back?" Maga asked once they were both clean and tucked up in their respective beds.

Now that he was here, the darkness didn't seem as edgy.

Everything looked the same again, the way it used to. She could feel her eyelids growing heavier as she struggled to stay awake long enough to hear his answer.

"Dunno, I just knew I had to come back."

"And Grandma didn't mind?"

"No…it was strange, like she was pleased I decided to come back."

"That is strange," Maga said. It was the last thing she could remember before her thoughts turned black and she fell into sleep, weighted with the exhaustion and anxieties of the day.

In the morning, she woke abruptly and sat up, her heart thumping. "Doxin?"

Looking around, there was no evidence that last night wasn't just a dream. His bed was neatly made, looking as untouched as it was yesterday. Throwing back the covers, Maga leapt out of bed and bounded out onto the porch.

"Doxin?"

There was no answer. Maga's gaze swung out around the clearing. She didn't see him anywhere or any sign that he was actually back. Shoulders slumped, Maga headed towards the communal room where she would have her breakfast, alone. Suddenly she wasn't very hungry. At least there was one less day for her to worry about.

"Were you looking for me?" Doxin asked as she swung open the door.

"Doxin! I was calling and calling for you."

He stood, a bemused look on his face as he stirred one of their chipped ceramic bowls with a spoon. 'I'm right here.'

"I thought maybe last night was a dream and you weren't really here," Maga said, sliding onto one of the chairs.

"Well, it wasn't and I'm still here."

"Good, there're still two chores left on my list."

Doxin groaned. "I should have known better. You aren't glad to see me, you just wanted your slave back."

"That's not true at all," Maga pouted. "But you're better at crushing the mallow leaves."

"Fine. After breakfast I'll help. What's the other thing you need to do?"

"Just the milkweed roots." Doxin made a face when he heard the name milkweed. "See, I was being nice, I know you don't like chewing them."

"They're *your* chores. I shouldn't be helping at all."

"What would you do while I was busy, then? It's just to keep you from getting bored."

Doxin rolled his eyes but didn't reply. She could see he was making the thin pancakes he knew how to make so well. Maga didn't know where he learned it, certainly neither she nor Grandma could make a reasonable pancake but it was Doxin's specialty. He must have been glad to see her too.

Once they'd eaten, the two of them retired to the workroom where Maga had laid out the milkweed roots and the mallow leaves yesterday. The pile of leaves was much larger than the roots but she knew it would take them roughly the same amount of time to finish. Chewing roots was difficult work and afterwards her jaw would ache for hours.

"What do we do once we're done?" Doxin asked as he dragged the stool closer to the table so he could reach the stone mortar and pestle easier.

"I guess we can do whatever we want," Maga said with a shrug.

She hadn't really thought about it. Since agreeing to become a swamp witch when she was eight, Maga and Doxin rarely had time for games. She wasn't sure she'd know what to do with free time.

Maga scooped the roots off the table, rolling them up in an apron and carrying them over to Grandma's rocking chair. With a jar next to her on the ground, ready for the chewed roots to be deposited in, the two began the long tasks in front of them.

Even though she always hesitated over the first root, the taste both acrid and slightly sweet, a combination that set her teeth on edge, Maga quickly fell into the pattern of it. Chewing roots was dull work and she couldn't talk much while she was at it, not wanting to swallow any of the juices. Doxin tried to keep up a running, mostly one-sided conversation, but not being able to participate dulled her interest.

So when a voice called from outside the clearing, Maga was all too ready to answer. Spitting the mashed root into the jar, Maga climbed to her feet, wiping her face off on the apron.

"Maga, what do we do?" Doxin hissed, staring at her over his shoulder, his arm no longer moving.

"We gotta see what they want. You stay here."

"Stay here? You don't even know who it is."

"But if it's someone bad, you can surprise them."

Doxin didn't look convinced but Maga was already out the door. Following the voice led Maga to the edge of the clearing. Through a thick screen of leaves she could almost make out the person on the other side.

"Can I help?" Maga called, wanting to make sure she was heard.

"We need to see the swamp witch, it's urgent," a childish voice replied, quivering with some emotion.

Maga didn't know what to say. Grandma wouldn't be back for at least a day. "She's busy," Maga ended up saying, biting her lip and hoping that would work.

"But we *need* her."

Maga paused. It did sound urgent. "What's wrong?"

"My brother's hurt. One of the heads got him while we were hunting. He needs help."

"What kind of hurt?" Maga asked, shifting from foot to foot. She didn't know how to fix too many hurts but she didn't want to turn someone away if she could do anything.

"I don't- can't you just…" The frustration and anxiety was too obvious for Maga to ignore.

"Ok, bring him through," Maga said.

"How? The bushes are all…oh!"

Maga pulled aside the bushes and leaves, creating a clear path through to the clearing. She didn't even notice the strain on her will as she normally did when she tried to manipulate the swamp like Grandma, instead focusing on the girl's voice and the boy's pain. Both hovered outside her own awareness of herself.

The small girl looked surprised when she saw Maga but didn't say anything, instead, dragging her brother through the path Maga cleared. She didn't know how the girl managed this far, the boy so much older and bigger, crushing his younger sister.

"Here, let me help," Maga said, ducking under his other arm. The boy groaned and twitched away.

"No, you can't touch…he's hurt there," the sister babbled.

"Then let me take your place. You must be exhausted."

Maga thought the sister only allowed her to in hopes of hurrying it all along. Maga slipped under the boy's other shoulder and hoisted him as best she could. Walking backwards, his sister looked on, wringing her hands and warning Maga to be careful, don't hurt him.

Doxin came to see what was going on and Maga was glad to see him. He hadn't stayed hidden like she told him to but he rarely did what she wanted over what he wanted. When he saw her struggling, Doxin jumped off the porch to help.

"You can't touch that side," Maga told him.

Doxin backed away as Maga and the brother tried to get up the steps. Though he was conscious, their injured guest wasn't very coherent. He mumbled and moaned but at least he tried to help, putting one foot in front of the other. But when the stairs presented a challenge too big for him, Doxin stepped in.

"Go on in, Maga, I've got him," Doxin said, shooing her away.

Maga did as she was told, ducking out from under the boy's arm. She grabbed the sister, only a few years younger than herself, and pulled her into the workroom. Once the girl was safely sitting as far away from the action as she could be, Maga started preparing for their guest. Grandma had a slab at the back of the workroom where the occasional visitor was put. It was also the same place Maga would undergo her surgery when she was old enough.

Throwing a blanket over top, Maga turned when she heard Doxin at the door. She ran over to pull it open for him and he limped in, heavily loaded down with the body of their injured stranger.

"Over here, bring him over here."

Maga herded Doxin and helped him ease his burden onto the table. Once he was up there, they both stood back and looked on. Maga didn't even know where to begin. She knew some rudimentary healing, Grandma drilled her in ever herb and its uses as they dried or chopped or boiled it. That didn't mean she'd ever practice their uses before.

"Where's the swamp witch?" the sister interrupted Maga's spiraling doubts.

Maga and Doxin looked at each other. "She isn't here," Maga said finally.

"What do you mean she isn't here?" the girl cried, bouncing out of her seat. "You said she was busy!"

"She *is* busy, that's why she isn't here," Doxin replied, crossing his arms over his chest and frowning down at the little girl.

"I'm her apprentice," Maga said, hoping that might mean something though the words sounded hollow to her.

She didn't know where the word apprentice came from. Grandma certainly never called her that but it was an echo in a buried memory and it sounded like the right word to use.

"Then do something!"

Maga took a deep breath, trying to remember how she'd seen Grandma deal with patients. She would start with questions.

"Can you tell me what happened?" Maga asked.

"I already did. We got attacked by heads while we were hunting. He's been bitten."

"Ok," Maga said. Obviously questions weren't going to help here.

She turned her back on the fuming girl, stepping closer to her patient. She didn't know if he could wait for Grandma to return but it sounded straightforward, just a few bites. Maybe she would be able to handle it on her own, or do enough to keep him alive until Grandma got back.

The boy's shirt was stained red so she couldn't tell exactly where he was bitten. Grabbing a knife from the work table, Maga slipped it in through a tear on his shirt and cut it off, peeling it away from the angry wounds underneath. His side was a mess of blood and torn flesh and she wrinkled her nose, almost gagging on the scents.

"What are you doing? Don't you hurt him!"

Maga heard a scuffle behind her. Doxin held their guest back, the girl's eyes wild as she scrabbled to get closer.

"Can you take her out of here?" Maga asked him. She couldn't work with her patient's sister in the room. She knew she would have to hurt the boy to help him.

Maga peeled the rest of the shirt off, trying to find any other wounds. It was mostly his side but his arm had a chunk taken out as well. Taking several deep breaths, Maga tried to calm her mind so she could think clearly.

Grandma always left sterilized water in several jugs. Whenever she used some, the old woman immediately made enough to fill up the jugs again. There was nothing worse than a patient waiting on clean water.

Maga found one of the jugs and dragged it closer to her patient. With the small scoop inside the jug, Maga pulled some out and ladled it onto her patient's wounds. Cleaning them out would allow her to see the damage more clearly. She poured until it ran pink, no brown or green mixed in. Her patient thrashed and moaned from the very first drop but Maga gritted her teeth against the sounds he made and kept pouring.

When it was done she tidied the jug away, ignoring the soaked floor, and stepped closer to the table, peering down at the wound in his side. She could see the tear marks where the teeth had been but it didn't look as bad as she thought. The wounds were shallower than she hoped for. But her patient shivered and moaned even when she wasn't touching him. Reaching up, Maga laid the back of her hand across his forehead. A fever.

She frowned. It was probably too early for an infection and the wounds all looked clear but a fever might mean complications she couldn't deal with. Trying to push the negative thoughts to the back of her head, Maga turned towards the shelves where Grandma kept the herbs. Maga knew them inside and out, as filling and keeping them full was her responsibility.

Pulling arnica and belladonna down from the shelves, Maga put them onto the work table before rooting around for the swamp cabbage leaves they used for wrapping wounds and making poultices.

"Hey, Maga, you doing ok?" Doxin asked from the doorway.

"Yeah, fine, sure," Maga replied, distracted.

"You don't sound too fine."

She heard him slip inside the room. "What'd you do with the sister?"

"She's sleeping in the communal room. I thought you might need help."

Like Maga, Doxin trained with Grandma. It was one of the advantages to having a human familiar. He leaned over her shoulder, staring down at what she was doing. She could feel his eyes and almost hear his thoughts buzzing as he assessed her plan.

Together they worked to alleviate their patient's pain. Doxin crushed Belladonna leaves with a basic salve Grandma kept. Once he was done, Maga slathered the result over the open wounds, sealing it with arnica leaves and finally, the swamp cabbage leaves.

"Do you think that will work?" Doxin asked.

"He has a fever. I don't know if it's an infection or not."

"Is that why you wanted to use belladonna?"

"Yeah."

Doxin laid a hand on her shoulder as they stared at their patient. Shadows stretched across the room, the sun setting. She hadn't realized it was so late. Where the day had gone, she couldn't say.

"I'll go make us some dinner," Doxin told her.

"Ok," Maga replied, not really hearing him. The boy in front of her was sweating again.

Maga grabbed the blanket from the back of the rocking chair and threw it over him, careful not to touch his dressings. She found a clean cloth and dunking it into one of the jugs of water, Maga mopped his brow. He moaned at the touch of the cold water, reaching up his good arm to clasp her hand and the cloth to his head.

"How you feeling?" Maga whispered.

He moaned but didn't say anything. With her hand stuck, Maga inched closer, trying to make it more comfortable for her arm to hang, suspended. She ignored the ache as she continued to hold the cloth to his forehead, even when Doxin came back, a plate in one hand.

"You not eating with me?" Maga asked when she saw only one plate.

"Carly woke up," Doxin told her as if that explained everything.

It must have because he dropped the plate off and left again. Maga looked over at the weak stew he prepared, a cut of bread sticking out of it. Her stomach roiled and she looked away.

"Water," her patient croaked.

Maga jerked, surprised to hear his voice. Leaving the cloth draped over his forehead, she scrambled for the jug of water and something clean for him to drink out of. Her patient hissed when she eased his head up to let him drink but he greedily swallowed the water, quite a bit of it splashing down the sides of his face. He only laid his head back down when it was all gone.

She could feel him watching her as she turned to put the water down. When she spun back around, his eyes assessed her face. Brown eyes like hers danced over her features.

"You don't look like a witch," he said, pausing for breath in between almost every syllable.

Maga didn't know how to reply. If she told him she wasn't the swamp witch, he might doubt her. One of the first things Grandma taught her was the importance of a person's attitude and thoughts in their recovery. They had to have faith and trust. They had to be positive.

But staring into those soft warm eyes, Maga also didn't want to lie. She felt suddenly shy and not at all like herself. Twisting a lank of hair in between her fingers, she blushed.

"So, how do I look? Will I survive?" he asked, trying to look down at his wounds. He stretched too far and fell back with a cry, panting as pain caused him to break out in another sweat.

"You mustn't move," Maga told him, stepping forward. She wrung out the wet cloth, dipped it again and replaced it on his forehead. She dragged it over his face and neck, hoping to cool him down. At least he was talking.

"I'm so tired," he said with a sigh, closing his eyes. Maga didn't know if that was good or bad, trying to keep the alarm from blooming too rapidly in her chest. "You won't leave me, will you?" he asked, capturing her hand.

"Of course not," Maga told him.

She let him hold her hand until he fell asleep. Once she knew he wouldn't wake if she moved, Maga fetched the stool, dragging it up to the slab her patient slept on. Perching, she reached out and grabbed his hand, holding it gently between hers. She didn't know if she'd be able to sleep all night, waiting for Grandma to come back and take control. She thought the boy would last until then but fear kept her eyes from closing all night.

Even as the morning sun streamed through the windows, Maga kept her eyes on her patient's face. He tossed and turned most of the night, waking to delirium when Doxin came in to see why she wasn't in bed. Maga mopped his brow and changed his dressing but he didn't speak again. She hoped infection hadn't set in and that Grandma would be back soon.

Maga didn't even know exactly where her mentor was. She didn't know when the old woman would be back. Doxin was no help either. He knew as little as she. They hadn't made it anywhere by the time Doxin decided to turn around and come back.

The door creaked and Maga whirled to see who it was. But it

was only Doxin and not Grandma. She sighed and turned back to the pale face of her patient.

"How's Tate doing?" Doxin asked.

"Tate?"

"That's his name."

"Oh."

Maga tried to fit the name to the face in front of her. She wasn't sure if it sounded or looked right. Tate. It was good to have a name for him though. She should have thought to ask earlier.

"So, how's he doing?" Doxin asked again when she didn't reply the first time.

"I don't know," Maga said. "He's feverish and he hasn't spoken since last night. He'll only take a little water but his wounds don't look any worse. I can't see any signs of infection and the bites aren't any hotter than they should be."

"Will he hang on 'til Grandma gets back?"

"He has to. It was just a few bites. People don't die over a few bites, not when they come to the swamp witch."

"But you aren't the swamp witch."

"That doesn't mean I shouldn't be able to help," Maga cried. "It's a simple thing!"

"I know it seems simple, but wounds like this can be tricky," Doxin said soothingly. "Grandma's had years and years of experience on you."

"But it's morning and she still isn't back."

"Do you want me to go look for her?"

"No! Then I'll be all alone."

"I'll just go keep Carly occupied then," he told her.

Maga nodded miserably, selfishly wishing he could stay here and tell her it would be alright.

The day passed as slowly as yesterday passed quickly. She didn't want to believe it when the sky turned a dark red and once again, the shadows threw their weight round the room, shrouding it in darkness.

Tate seemed to being doing better, sleeping easier though she was worried that he hadn't woken much during the day. Her vision was a little grey around the edges so when he drifted off into what seemed to be a peaceful sleep, Maga scooted over to the latest meal Doxin left at the work table.

Once she'd eaten, Maga could hardly keep her eyes open. Drowsy from so little sleep and woozy from so little food, she found it hard to fight her body's needs much longer. Shaking herself, she paced around the room, trying to stay awake. If she fell asleep now she might not notice if something happened to Tate during the night. She still didn't know where Grandma was but since the old woman wasn't back on the third day as she promised, Maga could hardly count on her to show up.

When she felt a little more awake, Maga resumed her seat next to Tate. She refreshed the damp cloth and tucked the blanket up a little higher. After a quick check under the dressing, and satisfied that she couldn't see or feel any signs of infection, Maga settled in for another long vigil.

But an hour after full darkness had fallen, Maga could feel sleep tugging at her, a fight she couldn't win. Her dreams were strange and fraught with dangers, disappointments and still more shadows. But a rough hand on her shoulder, shaking her, cut through them like a knife. She sat up, gasping. Her hand was ensconced in Tate's but the boy was still asleep.

A dark shadow loomed over her and she fell off the stool with a squeak.

"Shh, it's ok, girl. Just me. Why don't you go to bed, I'll take good care of him," Grandma said.

Maga stood slowly, her legs wobbly beneath her. "I can't go to bed. I can't sleep. I have to be here in case something happens."

"Then go sit in the rocking chair, I'll be right here, watching him for you."

Sleep-fogged, Maga nodded and plodded over to the rocking chair. Curling up in it, she kept her eyes glued to Grandma's shadowy form and Tate's face, touched by a ray of moonlight. Grandma placed Tate's hand back on the slab. She leaned over his prone form, one outstretched finger running over his body, an inch of air separating them.

Even when she nodded off, Maga could still see Grandma's image flickering behind her eyelids, that one finger sweeping down the length of Tate, hovering above his body. She wanted to stay awake to tell Grandma about the fever, the delusion and the strange lack of infection causing those problems but she couldn't move her thoughts to her mouth.

Maga blinked after what seemed seconds, squinting at the bright sunlight. Grandma was still there, as she'd promised, sitting on the stool next to the slab where Tate had lain the night before, knitting. Maga sat up, rocking the chair backwards with the force of it, turning in place, trying to find Tate.

"Where is he?" Maga asked, springing to her feet.

"The boy?" Grandma asked, not looking up from her knitting.

"Yes! He was right there last night, I know he was. And he had a fever, he wasn't talking..." Then a horrible thought stuck Maga. She covered her mouth with one hand, her eyes wide and terrified. "Did he...did he die?"

Grandma laughed, one of her full-bellied laughs that carried through the room. Putting her knitting down on the slab, Grandma got to her feet.

"He's fine," the old woman reassured Maga.

But Maga was not about to let her mentor dismiss her like that. "Where is he? He could barely drink yesterday let alone move around."

"He got much better. You did very well," Grandma said approvingly.

"Where is he?"

"He's having breakfast with his sister and Doxin. Carly was very worried about him and I thought it best that they have some time together so that they both could see how well he was getting on."

"But he wasn't getting on well. Did you fix him? How did you do it?"

"No, I didn't fix him," Grandma said, shaking her head.

"You didn't?"

"No, my girl, you did."

"How did I fix him? I thought he was gonna die!"

"Well, he didn't. I didn't even need to do anything. I watched him all night, got him water when he asked for it, but nothing else."

"I don't understand," Maga said, twisting her hands in her dress.

Grandma shuffled a little closer and threw her arm around Maga's hunched shoulders. She ducked her head close to Maga's.

"You don't have to. A witch doesn't always understand her own witchery at first. It doesn't need to make sense to you for it to work on others."

"You mean I fixed him with my witchery?" Maga hadn't heard anything like that before. Grandma rarely spoke of witchery, saying that much of their work depended on practicality.

"You did."

Maga paused to think about that. She didn't know how she fixed him with her witchery. She didn't feel anything different, she didn't do anything strange.

"Why didn't you come home yesterday like you said you would?" Maga asked eventually.

If her witchery hadn't worked out, Tate could have been very poorly off by the time Grandma showed up. In fact, Maga had thought he was.

"I did come back yesterday. It wasn't yet midnight."

Maga scowled. "That's not what you said when you said two days. That was more like three! Really bad stuff could have happened. It nearly did."

"I let Doxin come back," Grandma told her, as if that was a gift Maga should be thankful for.

"Fat lot of good he did," she grumbled. "I barely saw him."

"Well, I knew what was going on and the woodpecker assured me you were handling everything just fine."

Grandma turned towards the door where her woodpecker familiar, hopped into sight. Maga briefly wondered, not for the first time, if he had a name.

"How would *he* know?" Maga asked angrily.

She and Grandma's familiar didn't get on very well though she didn't know why. She'd saved his life years ago and she expected him to be more grateful than he'd been.

"He's been a witch's familiar for longer than you've been alive. Besides," Grandma added in an offhand manner, "he can see magic."

"What?"

"He can see magic," Grandma repeated.

"Can *you* see magic?" Maga asked.

She didn't know magic was something you could see. She knew so little about the very stuff she was supposed be learning to master.

"Not as well as he can, and not from as far either."

"Wow."

"So, I knew there wasn't any rush to get back home. You had

everything under control."

"Was this all a test?" Maga asked suspiciously as soon as it occurred to her.

Grandma grinned, her lips stretching back to show her perfectly straight, white teeth. She only laughed when Maga glared, planting her fits on her hips as she waited for an answer from Grandma.

"Every day is a test," Grandma replied.

"That's not what I meant and you know it," Maga shot back. "Was this a test?"

"You think I would do this to you?" Grandma asked.

Maga thought for a brief second. "Of course you would."

There was very little she thought Grandma wouldn't do if it served her purposes.

"Well, then it's a good thing Tate's doing just fine."

"You didn't answer my question," Maga said accusingly. The lack of sleep and food and Grandma's cavalier attitude were combining in a dangerous fashion.

Grandma didn't respond. She just patted Maga on the head, ignoring the conversation. 'We should go see how everyone's getting on,' Grandma said.

The old woman strode out of the room, her woodpecker fluttering to her shoulder. Maga watched Grandma leave, feeling torn between anger and relief. Even if it wasn't a test, she felt like she'd proved something, if only to herself. Pulling herself together, Maga hurried after Grandma, eager to see how her patient was getting on.

The Pick of the Swamp

"One eye too many…" Grandma tutted. "I told them, didn't I?"

Maga wasn't sure if she was supposed to answer. She tried to sit up straighter. Grandma had her perched on a stool in the workroom. She was accustomed to Grandma's muttered conversations with herself. It was rare that anyone else could understand them. Even after a decade with the old woman, Maga barely understood anything the woman did or said.

"Sit up, eyes front."

Maga widened her brown eyes, staring into Grandma's mismatched ones. The wooden walls of the hut blurred into a brown background. Sheaths of herbs and plants hung from the ceilings and the slanted shelves held many things, some Maga knew intimately and others she could only guess at.

"Better," Grandma conceded. The old woman tottered around the stool, muttering to herself. A lot of it was a farce. Maga had seen Grandma move as quickly and as smoothly as a water snake. But there were images to maintain, even just between the two of them.

"How old are you again?" Grandma asked for the fourth time that day. It was the first thing she'd asked when Maga sat down to breakfast in the communal room.

"Seventeen," Maga answered once more.

She knew what was coming. She'd known since she was eight. She was going to become a witch.

"Yes, that's about right." Grandma came full circle again to stand in front of Maga. Her crinkled grey hair was pulled up in a bun, sitting precariously on the top of her head. Grandma leaned in, peering in first one eye and then the other. Maga stared back.

"Have you thought about it?" Grandma asked.

"Of course," Maga responded.

She'd thought about every day since she learned what awaited her. At a young age she'd been equally excited and revolted by her future. Now that it was almost upon her, Maga dreaded it but her sick fascination with Grandma's round, beetle-black eye meant she never wanted anything else.

She'd been preparing herself for this day.

"Well? What is it, girl?" Grandma asked impatiently.

"Alligator."

"What?" Grandma's fierce scowl didn't deter Maga.

"Alligator," Maga repeated.

"I heard you the first time, girl." Grandma crossed her skinny arms over her chest and stepped back, frowning as she stared at Maga.

"I thought I could choose anything," Maga said. It was private choice and one she hadn't shared with Grandma up until today.

"You can," Grandma said. "But normally you'd choose what I chose."

"Why?"

Maga hadn't heard that before. This was a ritual they rarely discussed. Maga didn't know many of the details, she always assumed Grandma would share them when she needed to know more about it.

"It's easier," Grandma sniffed.

Maga didn't reply. She knew what she wanted. Besides, she didn't have the luxury of sharing a set of eyes with her familiar. Nothing would ever make her take away Doxin's beautiful blue eyes. Not even so she could have one herself.

"You do know that alligator eyes don't fit as well in our eye sockets," Grandma warned. Her own mismatched eye looked shrunken into her face.

Maga had spent a long time stalking alligators, trying to see if it was even feasible. She'd never heard of someone trying it before but that wasn't going to stop her. The gator eye was more similar to the human eye than the bird one Grandma had.

"I don't care," Maga said stubbornly.

"Don't go into this blind," Grandma said. "It's a big decision and I think you need to take some time and see what else is out there. You've been stuck on this gator idea for a long time."

Maga stared at the old woman. "I never said-"

"You didn't need to. Do you think I'm stupid, girl?"

Maga slumped on the stool.

"I want you to pick three animals, and tell me why they would be easier, better choices."

Maga groaned.

"And I don't want any attitude," Grandma scowled.

Maga rolled her eyes but nodded.

"Alright, you can go," Grandma dismissed Maga.

The teen hopped off the stool and fled for the fresher swamp air. They lived in three wooden houses, shoved together so that they propped each other up. The land the buildings stood on was solid and closed in by trees and thick bushes. Sometimes it seemed like safety; at others, a prison.

At least she had Doxin. She'd found him nine years ago, at the start of her journey down the path that would lead her to her destiny. He was the catalyst. He was her familiar.

"Maga!" Doxin called out. She whipped around, trying to find him.

"Up here!" Doxin was high up in the trees that arched over the clearing. Dangling, he grinned at her through a thin screen of leaves. It was impossible not to smile back.

"Come down from there! I don't want you breaking that fool neck of yours!" Maga said, laughing.

"Aww, but Grandma…" Doxin said, a name he always called her when she got too bossy, as he swung down to land on the ground. He marched up to meet her in the middle of the clearing. "So, how did it go? Was it actually today?"

Maga and Doxin both knew something was up when Grandma asked Maga twice at the breakfast table how old she was.

"It was today," Maga said with a nod. "But she wasn't happy with my decision."

Maga frowned, still unsure why Grandma wasn't thrilled. It didn't matter to the old woman, or it shouldn't. Each witch had the right to choose their eye. It made the pain easier to bear.

"Gators, right?"

Maga hadn't told Doxin either, but her fascination with the leathery creatures was hard to ignore. If anyone would have known, it would have been Doxin. They'd spent more time together than she could count, perched in the trees above the gator pool, watching.

"Yeah," Maga sighed.

"So, why wasn't she happy?"

Doxin's black curls were neater than Maga's brown ones. The curls hung straight and true, no matter how long his hair got. Maga's hair had a proclivity for knotting at the slightest provocation.

"I don't know, she said something about me being hung up on it…"

"Well, she wouldn't be wrong," Doxin said. He grinned when she glared at him, unrepentant.

"Yeah, well, now I have to find three other animals and tell her why each of them is a better choice."

"That'll be easy," Doxin replied. When Maga gave him a questioning look, he explained. "Well, there's the hawk, that'd be a great one. A snake, not sure which kind but that wouldn't be too hard to pick, and then something else."

"Hmm, that does sound easy," Maga said, considering.

She chewed her lip. There was no choice but to give in and do as Grandma said. With Doxin's help it wouldn't be too onerous a chore.

"Do you have to do a presentation for her?" Doxin asked.

"Something like that, I'm sure."

"So she can't think that you spent five minutes on it."

"Nope."

Maga would indulge the old woman because she had to and because Doxin looked excited at the prospect of the assignment. But that didn't mean she would change her mind. Nothing would change her mind.

"Okay, so what we'll do is go find each of the animals, have a look-see and then in a few days, you can speak to Grandma again."

"That sounds like a decent plan," Maga agreed. "Now all we need to do is strategize," Maga said, grabbing his arm and pulling him through the hedge.

After so many years here, and with a lot of practice, Maga had mastered the foliage that surrounded the clearing. She couldn't do much in the swamp beyond but at least the thorns and bushes responded to her will as she mentally pulled them aside to create a path. It didn't even take much thought anymore, having become second-nature to her.

Not far from the clearing sat a small island with a leaning tree on it. It was their tree and it was the best place to think and argue and plan and play. Maga swung up into it first, Doxin following quickly behind. They climbed up as far as they could, as far up as the tree would support their weight.

"So we need to find a hawk," Maga said when they caught their breath once again. Doxin nodded. "And a snake?"

"Yeah, I think she'll like that and it makes sense for a swamp," Doxin said.

He hadn't originally come from the swamp but after almost a decade, he'd adjusted as if he'd been born here.

"Yeah, we could do a poisonous one! She'd love that," Maga said, getting into it.

It was an adventure, something she hadn't had in a long time. While there was interest in training to be a witch, it mostly consisted of memorization, herbs and willpower. She learned new ways to see the world and situations but there was little excitement and this next step would provide it in spades.

"What about the last one?" Doxin asked.

"I don't know. What do you think?" Maga asked.

She'd never considered another animal before and even though this was more of a hypothetical exercise to appease Grandma, Maga still struggled to think of what else would be appropriate for her.

"A toad?" Doxin didn't look sure about his suggestion even as he said it.

"A toad?" Maga echoed.

"It's small. That's certainly something useful, isn't it?"

"I suppose … a snake is pretty small though," Maga said. She didn't think she could convince Grandma she thought a toad would be a better donor than a gator.

"Well, it's smaller, a lot more harmless than the other two as well. I think she'll want you to look at three different animals. If you have three big predators then you aren't doing this the way she means you to," Doxin argued, his palms scraping against the bark of the tree.

Maga sighed. "Ok, fine. It doesn't matter that much anyways, it's not like I'm going to change my mind," Maga said. She'd had her heart set on an alligator eye since she knew she'd undergo the surgery.

"You can't go into it thinking like that," Doxin said.

Maga scowled at him. "Not you too," she said.

"No, not me too. I'm on your side, I've always been."

"I know," Maga said with a smile. "You have to be. You're my familiar."

"I'm your friend," Doxin replied. It was an argument they use to have as children and by now it was so worn it was more of a joke. They smiled at each other.

"Fine, then what should we find first?" Maga asked.

They decided the hawk would be hardest to find and so should be the first on their list. After deciding which animals to stalk, Maga and Doxin took the rest of the day off. They were relaxed and laughing when they sat down to dinner with Grandma that night. She didn't ask them anything about their day and didn't bring up the conversation she had with Maga that morning. It was one of the easier meals they'd shared with her.

"So, tomorrow?" Doxin asked from his bed.

"Tomorrow," Maga agreed. She smiled in the dark, pleased to have an adventure waiting for her the next morning. She got over the disappointment of having to wait for the surgery. She could put off the pain for a bit longer.

She fell easily asleep and woke at the first dim ray of light. Sitting up quickly, Maga jumped out of bed to go wake Doxin. She wanted to get an early start to the day. He protested when she leapt onto his bed, shaking him, but got up and followed her to breakfast.

Maga gobbled the food Grandma placed in front of them, just shoveling it into her mouth, barely taking the time to chew. Grandma watched the two of them with shrewd eyes but didn't say anything.

"Are you ready, Doxin?" Maga asked, her plate empty in front of her. Doxin was still eating and looked up at her, his cheeks bulging.

"Big plans for the day?" Grandma asked mildly.

"Just a bit of exploring," Maga replied. "Was there anything you needed me for?"

"You can have a few days off," Grandma said.

"Really?" Doxin asked, beating Maga to it.

"There's not much more Maga can do at this level," Grandma shrugged.

"What's that supposed to mean?" Maga asked, her brows snapping together over her eyes.

"You need to complete the next step."

"The surgery," Maga said.

Grandma climbed to her feet, her black eye sparkling. Maga and Doxin watched the old woman leave the room, her familiar following close behind. Maga scowled at her teacher's back and Doxin snickered at her.

"What?" Maga asked, whirling around to glare at her own familiar.

"Nothing. Just thinking how alike you two are," Doxin replied.

"We're nothing alike."

"If you say so," Doxin said with a smile.

"Let's just get going," Maga replied.

"Can't I finish my breakfast first?" Doxin asked, protesting.

"Fine," Maga sighed.

She sat and watched him as he slowly ate his way through the bird eggs on his plate and the frittatas Grandma made. Her leg jumped of its own accord, her fingers tapping on the table. She could tell it annoyed Doxin but she couldn't stop herself. She wanted to be outside already, looking for that hawk. She needed to complete the assignment before Grandma would allow her to continue in the steps towards complete witchery.

"Are you done yet?" Maga asked once his plate was clean.

"We should probably clean up-"

"No! Grandma gave us a couple days off. That means chores too." Maga grabbed Doxin's arm and pulled him out of the communal room, onto the porch and into the clearing before he could put off their adventure any longer.

"Slow down," Doxin shouted as they ran through the hedge too quickly for it to pull back fully.

Maga heard him but didn't listen, just concentrated on retracting the thorns faster. Soon they were sloshing through the waters of the swamp as Maga hurried them further and further from the clearing and the house within it.

"Maga-"

"Shh," Maga shushed her familiar, her eyes darting around the tree tops.

They'd slowed to a walk but every once in a while she stopped completely, trying to see if she could spot a hawk circling overhead. The familiar screech was missing but that didn't mean the hawks weren't nearby.

"I know there's a family of them somewhere," Maga muttered. Of course the one day she actually needed to find them, they hid from her. So many times before they'd scared off her own prey or stole something she'd hunted down.

"It isn't supposed to be easy," Doxin whispered.

She dropped his arm finally, turning to glare. He glared right back, unapologetic. Maga carried on, walking and stopping, listening for the hawk's cry. She turned them at one point, circling around the clearing Grandma's house stood in. The hawks made their presence known not far outside the clearing just about every day. She knew they were around somewhere.

"Maga, I don't think we're going to find them today. Can't we just get a snake or a toad and leave the hawk until it wants to be found?"

"That's not how this is going to work," Maga growled. Her eyes were tired but they searched the treetops anyway.

"We've been at this for hours. Can't we at least stop and get something to eat?"

"You can if you want. I'm going to keep looking."

Doxin didn't reply. He merely sighed and kept following, shading his eyes as he looked skywards. Maga didn't pay much attention to him after that. Unless he spoke, her attention needed to be concentrated on her prey.

Only when the sun started to set did Doxin decide they both really needed to go home.

"You can't even see in the dark. There's no point carrying on," Doxin told her, his weariness showing in his voice.

"The sun's not gone yet," Maga replied stubbornly.

"You aren't going to win at everything."

"I know that."

"Then let's go home and try again tomorrow. You know they live around here, they can't hide forever."

Maga capitulated in the end. She didn't want to admit it but Doxin was right. Besides, walking around the swamp in the dark was stupid, she could almost hear Grandma's voice in her head telling her so. While the old woman never laid down rules for Maga or Doxin, her withering look whenever they mentioned doing something stupid stuck with her.

"Aren't you going to come in for dinner?" Doxin asked when Maga turned away from the communal room they shared meals in.

"No, I just want to go to bed."

"You need to eat," Doxin reminded her. "You haven't had anything since breakfast."

"I have stuff in my room," she said, walking away from him.

Maga shut her door to the porch behind her and collapsed in her bed. Rooting around in her bedside table for the food she stored there, and had done ever since Grandma sent her to her room without dinner when she was nine, Maga rolled over, stale crackers held in one hand.

After she ate, the crackers barely alleviating the pain in her stomach, Maga fell asleep, still holding the collection of crumbs in her hand. Not long after her eyes closed for that last time, Maga sat up in the bed, her heart thumping wildly in her chest, sweat cooling on her skin.

"Hello?" she called, her voice quiet.

She didn't know what prompted her to call out but there was the feeling that someone was in her room, someone that shouldn't be. Doxin used to sleep in here too but when they hit thirteen, Grandma decided he needed to move. Finally all three buildings were occupied.

"Anyone there?"

Maga groped for her knife, breathing easier when its familiar grip was in her hand. A snort at the doorway made her inhale. She froze, wondering what it was and why it hadn't attacked. When she didn't hear anything else, she shifted on the bed, closer to the wall, trying to see if the moonlight might answer her questions.

The door banged open and she saw something slither out of the room, onto the porch, before the door slammed shut again. Stilling her breath, Maga could hear the silence that said she was alone again. The house in the clearing was always safe and she could feel anger stirring that someone dared threaten that safety.

She scooted to the edge of the bed and touched down on the wooden floor. By now she knew exactly which boards creaked and which ones were safe to stand on. Opening the door carefully, she peered out onto the porch. The moonlight showed nothing unusual on the porch. The clearing looked empty as well.

Maybe someone else would have dismissed it all as a dream but Maga didn't. With her knife in hand, she stepped off the porch. The bushes around the edges of the clearing rustled off to her left and she swung around. Still there was nothing to see.

Carefully, Maga edged closer to the where she'd seen the movement, thankful that the moon was so bright. Through the foliage, she thought she could see the gleam of eyes but when she pulled aside the limb they were behind there was nothing there.

"Come out, come out," she called softly, feeling less like prey and more like a predator with every step.

She heard movement to her right and whirled to follow. The noises led her out of the clearing and into the swamp proper. Unafraid to follow, something about the moonlight and being out alone in the dark made her reckless, Maga plunged ahead, heedless of any danger.

In front of her she could see something, dodging and weaving through the waters of the swamp, quicker than should be possible. She panted trying to keep up until all traces of the thing disappeared entirely. Maga stood, silent as she looked around, trying to find where it might have gone.

A flutter out of the corner of her eye caught her attention and she lunged towards it. At the base of a tree, Maga found an injured hawk. When her shadow fell over it, the animal let out a sharp, fearful cry and shuddered. Next to it lay a black water snake, unmoving and a fat toad, pinned down under a stone.

Maga backed up slowly. Someone had collected the three animals for her, that much she knew. Why, she couldn't answer. A hiss broke her out of her stupor and she dashed for the animals, scooping them up carefully in her skirt, careful of the hawk's talons and sharp beak. But the bird didn't seem inclined to offer her harm, seeming more scared of her than anything else.

She reached out with a touch of her willpower to quiet all three of the animals. The snake was unconscious and the toad stunned. The hawk was the only one coherent.

"Shh, shh," Maga said as she hurried back towards the clearing. "You have nothing to fear from me," Maga told the bird.

At the sound of her voice and the touch of her mind, the bird quieted, panting. She could see its heartbeat thundering in its small chest and she moved a little quicker.

Once she made it the clearing, Maga crept through the bushes and thorns, glad that she could still pull them back with her will despite her distracted thoughts. Pausing on the edge of the foliage, Maga listened to see if she could hear anyone stirring. The moonlight told her it was still quite late at night, or so very early in the morning she needn't worry.

Knowing she couldn't store the animals in her room, Maga headed for Grandma's workroom. The old woman would have the stuff she needed to keep them safe and caged until Grandma got a look at them in the morning. The snake wriggled suddenly in her skirt and Maga tried not to shriek and drop all three of them. At least fear was keeping the toad silent and still, she didn't know how she'd catch it if it decided to leap. Her willpower was fading quickly and with it, any chance to control the animals any more.

The door got stuck under her hand but with a hefty push, Maga managed to get in, wincing at every sound she made. Before she put any of the animals down, she needed to find containers. The snake was easy. Grandma kept empty jars just in case she would need them and Maga slipped the water snake inside one, quickly dropping the lid down after it. The toad she placed in an upside down bowl.

With only the hawk left, Maga wrapped it a little more tightly up in her skirt, pressing it to her chest. It mewed anxiously but she ignored it. There had to be a birdcage sitting around somewhere. After a few minutes of quietly rattling around the workroom she knew by heart, Maga gave it up as a lost cause. She would have seen one before if Grandma had one.

Maga cast about for somewhere to put the hawk. The only place big enough and safe enough was the giant wardrobe that sat against one slanted wall. Maga opened it and peered in, relieved to see it had enough space for a medium, frightened bird.

Once inside, the bird lost whatever fear it had. Maga struggled to keep the cupboard shut as it banged against the inside doors. She reached for a broom, leaning up against the wardrobe and slipped it between the handles. Let the bird rage, it wouldn't escape.

Puffing, Maga looked around the room, satisfied with what she'd done. Whoever gave her the animals had done her a big favor while simultaneously freaking her out and making things more difficult. While the adventure of finding them might be gone, the surgery and the next step in her training was so much closer. With a quiet step, Maga left the room, still able to hear the dull thump of an angry hawk as she made her way back to her bedroom.

After that outing, Maga fell asleep easily, not even dreaming. She woke, refreshed and excited. It took her a moment to remember why and when she did, Maga couldn't help but grin. She bounced out of her bed and threw on a clean set of clothes, hurrying to the communal room. She couldn't wait to see the look on Grandma's face when Maga told her about the animals.

Only Doxin sat at the table this morning and when he saw her, the look on his face froze her feet at the threshold.

"What did you do?" he hissed.

"What do you mean?" Maga asked, creeping forward to join him at the table.

Over a spoonful of porridge, Doxin gave her an anxious look. "Grandma's furious about something and she was muttering about you. She didn't even eat this morning. She wants to see you in the workroom right now."

"But I haven't had breakfast," Maga protested.

"Maga! Didn't you hear me? Right now. She's furious."

"Ok, ok."

Maga stood, straightening her shirt and wiping off invisible lint. Rolling her shoulders back, she headed for the door. A last look at Doxin's face showed fear and she scowled. She hadn't done anything to make Grandma furious. Maybe he misread her mood.

But she still paused with her hand on the workroom door. Grandma frequently got mad or frustrated but she'd never seen the woman really lose her temper. The look on Doxin's face suggested she was about to see such a phenomenon.

When the door swung open under her hand, for once not sticking, the old woman glared. Standing in the middle of the room, Grandma clearly had been waiting for her.

"Sit," the old woman ordered brusquely, pointing to the stool Maga used.

Without a word, Maga slunk over to the stool and slid onto the smooth seat, her eyes not leaving the mismatched eyes of her mentor. The woman's human eye narrowed but the small, black eye didn't move.

"Well?" Grandma asked.

"Um…I don't…"

The frown deepened in the old woman's face, all her wrinkles sagging downwards in an echo. The frizzy hair on her head was standing up more than usual and the dark, bruised-looking bags under Grandma's eyes betrayed exhaustion but not weakness.

Without a word, Grandma stalked over to the wardrobe, withdrew the broom from the handles and threw open the doors. The hawk inside burst out, screeching as it circled over their heads, looking for a way out. It quickly realized there wasn't one and settled as closely to the door as it could get, its sharp eyes staring.

Maga didn't have a chance to speak before the lid on the jar holding the snake was yanked off, allowing the black snake to slither out, hissing. The flicker of its tongue told Maga just how angry it was and the bellow of a toad tore her attention away to the upended bowl. Grandma's hands were shaking with rage as she stood at her work table.

"What do you have to say for yourself?"

"I can explain! You know how you said I should find three other animals I might like instead of the alligator? Doxin and I decided these might be the best three and we spent all day looking for the hawk yesterday but we couldn't find one. There's a large family nearby but all day, I didn't hear a single one. So we came home and he said we should look tomorrow," Maga couldn't stop herself babbling as she told Grandma the whole story.

The woman's posture didn't change at all as Maga poured out her night time adventure. When she finished the story, Maga was breathing hard, her palms sweating. She didn't know what she'd done wrong. Maybe it wasn't the best idea trapping the animals overnight but it didn't do them any harm.

"So, you expect me to believe you just found them stunned or trapped and you brought them home?"

Maga nodded frantically. The old woman had to believe her. How could she make up such a stupid story? For it sounded stupid now that she heard it from her own lips.

"Do you know who would do something like that?" Grandma's voice was quiet but firm, the spark of anger still gleaming in her eyes.

Maga shook her head. She was bewildered by the whole thing. Obviously it wasn't Grandma and Maga knew it couldn't be Doxin, she would know if it was Doxin.

"Then I think you need to find out."

"How will I do that?" Maga hadn't even seen what it was last night, not a single conclusive glimpse.

"I'm sure you'll manage. I have no more use for you until you can tell me who did this and why." With that, Grandma turned her back on Maga, opening the door for the animals to flee into the swamp where they belonged.

Maga sat on the stool, shocked. She didn't know where to begin. When it became clear Grandma intended to ignore her, Maga slid off the stool and slipped out the door.

Doxin waited outside for her, his blue eyes large in his face. "Where did you get those animals so fast?"

"I don't know."

"Why was she so mad?"

"I'm not sure."

"What's going on?"

Maga huffed, her own temper rising now that she was out of the danger zone. "Last night, someone led me to a hawk, a snake and a toad. I brought them to Grandma but she was really angry."

"I thought that was what she wanted you to do…"

"So did I."

"Then…" Doxin cocked his head, his expression puzzled. He didn't even know what question to ask next, a feeling Maga could sympathize with.

"I have to find out who put them there and why."

"Ok…"

Doxin followed her off the porch and all the way to their tree. Maga swung up into the branches slowly, her mind trying to puzzle it out.

"So, what do we know?" Doxin asked once he was sitting next to her.

"I told you everything I know." She'd filled him in on their walk.

"You didn't see *anything* or hear *anything* that might give us a clue?"

Maga shook her head and let out a frustrated breath.

"All right," Doxin said, scrunching his face. "There has to be some logic to this."

Maga looked over at him. He handled logic and plans better than she did. Sometimes she thought that might be why he was her familiar, they complemented each other so well. Whatever other gifts he might have, she had yet to discover. The relationship between witch and familiar was delicate and individual. She only knew some of the gifts Grandma and her woodpecker shared.

"Someone obviously overheard us," Doxin said, breaking into her thoughts.

"They had to. I mean, it was only yesterday we even heard about Grandma's demands."

"And we were talking about it right here…"

"I'd like to think we'd notice someone eavesdropping."

"Could it have been Grandma?" Doxin asked, his tone telling her he knew how farfetched the idea was.

"Didn't you see her face this morning? There's no way it was her."

"Ok, ok, I had to ask."

They sat there in silence, trying to think of a solution.

"You can't talk to animals yet, can you?" Doxin asked hopefully.

Maga gave him a dirty look. "Don't you think you'd know if I could?"

"Well, we know Grandma can. Why doesn't she ask the hawk what happened?"

Maga's eyes widened at the suggestion. "That's a great idea!"

Doxin beamed.

Maga jumped down from the tree and hurried towards the clearing when a thought slowed her down. Doxin bumped into her, nearly sending them both sprawling.

"The hawk already left," Maga said.

"Oh. Do you think we could find it again?"

"We couldn't find one yesterday, what're our chances of finding the *exact same* hawk a day after it was already captured?"

"Slim to nil," Doxin sighed. "Do you think she asked them before she let them go?"

"Probably not. Why else send us out on this mystery mission?"

"Damn."

"Back to the tree," Maga ordered.

They turned back to the tree when a screech of anger caught her ears. Maga rushed towards the noise, stumbling over the hidden roots underneath the marshy surface of the swamp. Wedged in between two trees was a hawk struggling to break free. Maga stared down at it, amazed and bewildered. She heard Doxin behind her, could feel his breath on her shoulder as he stared down at the hawk too.

"Do you think it's the same one?" he asked.

She shook her head dumbly, unable to answer. Could it be a coincidence? She didn't think so.

"Can you go get Grandma?" Maga asked her familiar, trying to keep her voice as even as possible.

He didn't reply, only darted away. She waited with the hawk for him to come back with Grandma. Her mind whirled, trying to think what was going on. Someone seemed to be answering her every request. She wondered what else she might be able to wrangle from her mystery giver or what the motivation behind this all was.

"Stand aside, girl," Grandma ordered from behind her.

Maga sidestepped, unable to take her eyes of the hawk. It looked the same as the one she'd caught last night but in the dark and the fear of the morning, she hadn't gotten a very good look. Doxin stood next to her, slipping his hand into hers and squeezing.

Grandma bent down, leaning over the hawk. She stared into its frightened and angry eyes. When it saw her, the hawk stilled, though it continued to pant. A series of guttural noises erupted from its beak and Grandma listened carefully, nodding every once in a while before straightening up. She leaned over the branches holding the hawk down and pulled them apart. The hawk sprang out of its confinement, working its wings hard to clear the trees.

"What happened? Was that the same hawk?" Maga asked after a second of silence passed and she couldn't keep the questions in any longer.

"It was the same hawk," Grandma said as she turned around.

"And? What did it say?"

"It had a very interesting story to tell me."

Maga waited for Grandma to elaborate but the woman didn't.

"And?"

"And I think you need to figure out who's doing this and

why."

"But you already know?" Maga exploded.

"Yes."

Grandma shuffled past Maga and Doxin, obviously headed back to the house. Maga gaped as she watched the old woman go. Her gaze only shifted when Grandma called Doxin to her and, with an apologetic smile, Doxin followed.

Left alone to figure the mystery out, Maga stared down at the tree that held the hawk. She couldn't even begin to imagine who was doing this or why. She paced back and forth for a bit before growling and heading back to the tree she liked to think in. Sitting on the bottom branch, she wracked her brains for a way to discover the culprit.

"I want a sandwich," Maga announced after half an hour.

She watched the swamp under her, trying to see if anyone came to bring her a sandwich. Nothing and no one showed up. She frowned though she hadn't really expected it to be that easy.

Leaning back against the trunk of the tree, Maga closed her eyes. Maybe if she waited long enough, Grandma would take pity on her and give her a clue. Or, at least, give her Doxin back. Maga wasn't great with mysteries and the thought processes needed to solve them.

A rustle below her made her sit up, her eyes flying open. Peering down over the side of the branch, Maga saw something sitting on a stone at the base of the tree. Hopping down, she knelt to see what it was. It wasn't immediately obvious. She picked it up to look closer at it. Sandwiched between two large leaves of swamp cabbage was a dead fish.

Maga looked around, confused. Someone had left her a dead fish?

"Hello?"

No one answered her call.

"Is this my sandwich?" She couldn't think what else it might be.

Still no one answered and growling in frustration, Maga put the fish back down and shimmied up the tree. That wasn't a sandwich she could eat. Whoever it was must think that was hilarious. She wasn't amused at all.

Every time she made a request after that, it wasn't until she looked away purposefully that it was dropped off. Sometimes it took longer than others though she kept trying to think up something absurd to stump whoever it was. But without fail, her mystery giver found her a doll, a set of plates, a rusty old fishing rod and a new pillow.

"Maga?"

She sat up when she heard Doxin call her name.

"What is all this junk?" he asked as he saw the pile of stuff at the base of the tree.

"More presents," she told him sourly. "Has Grandma let you go?"

"No." He shrugged sheepishly and held up a small, covered basket. "Dinner," he said.

"Enough for two?"

"No, I'm to drop it off with you. Oh, and here's a blanket."

"I'm not allowed back until I know who it is?" Maga asked, outraged.

"I don't think so."

Maga dropped from the tree and snatched the blanket and basket with a scowl. Doxin smiled apologetically before turning and sauntering off into the swamp. She watched him go until the leaves swallowed his form. How Grandma thought she could do this was beyond her.

The answer only occurred to her as she began to drift off, surprisingly snug in the tree. Bolting upright, Maga asked for just about the only thing she hadn't thought of.

"I want to know who's doing this, right now," Maga demanded. She could have smacked herself for not thinking of it sooner.

At first nothing happened. The sky was still dimly lit by the setting sun and her eyes tried to pierce the foliage surrounding the island the tree sat on. It took a while but finally she heard the same rustling she'd been hearing all day. Three shady forms emerged from the bushes, half-sunken in the swampy waters.

"What? You?" Maga clutched the blanket to her chest, trying to make sense of the scene below her.

Three alligators slowly swam up to the island, their yellow eyes blinking up at her languidly. Their front feet set down on the dirt. One of them was clearly an adolescent but the other two were adults, one grizzled enough to make her gulp. Scars marked his hide, a fresh one gaping to show an empty eye socket.

"I don't understand…"

One of the gators growled at her. Somehow she knew what it wanted. Slinging the blanket over the tree limb, Maga slid down and joined them on the small island. She tried not to show any fear. For all her fascination and the many hours spent watching the alligators that lived nearby, she wasn't entirely comfortable facing them down. She wasn't as fearless as her younger self had been.

Grumbling noises from the middle gator were interrupted by the shrill whine of the adolescent. A scuffle erupted and the oldest gator took over, a rumbling growing in his stomach before oozing out through his teeth.

Maga stared down at them, still confused. She knew they were trying to tell her something but she didn't know how to speak to animals. Shaking her head to clear the fear and doubts away, Maga held up a hand.

"Wait, slow down. I can't understand you."

The largest alligator, with his scarred snout and single eye, beckoned her. She understood that at least. Edging closer, Maga got down on one knee. He snorted, breathing on her face. She scrunched her nose at the foul smell and he chortled. Coughing, she waved a hand in front of her nose, trying to dispel the smell.

The middle alligator tried again, growling at her and somehow, or because of the foul smelling breath, Maga understood what it was saying. Not in words, that's not the way they communicated, but in feelings.

She sat down, listening as the three of them tried to explain things to her. Bemused, she didn't make a sound. After a few minutes she was dismissed. Her fuzzy mind didn't allow any thoughts to break through as she walked back to the house, just as the gators told her to.

Though it was late enough for Grandma and Doxin to be in bed, the light on in the workroom told her Grandma must be waiting. As she opened the door, just as she thought, the older woman sat in her rocking chair.

"Well?" Grandma asked, looking up from the knitting needles and stretch of wool gathered between them.

Maga shook her head, trying to focus on Grandma's question

instead of the strangely domestic scene. "It was the gators," Maga said.

Grandma nodded in time to the rocking of her chair. "And?"

"The animals were presents. They wanted me to know how good they would be as allies and how honored to be chosen to give me an eye."

"I see. Did they say anything else?"

"They didn't mean to offend you with the animals."

"Uh huh. So, tell me why the hawk would be a better choice than an alligator."

Maga shifted on her feet, surprised by the question. "Well…" she paused, trying to bring her thoughts together from where they fled during the last twenty minutes. "Hawks can fly. They're also fierce. I wouldn't have to worry about being caught out without food."

"Ok. And the snake?"

"It's poisonous and small. Good at camouflage and sneaking up on things. I wouldn't have to worry about getting bit."

"And the toad?"

"Everyone overlooks a toad."

"And why is an alligator a bad idea?"

Maga didn't have an answer for that but she knew she had to say something. "They don't know what a sandwich is?"

Grandma frowned, not interested in humor, and clearly not understanding what she meant. Maga knew she had to try again.

"Um…they're unpredictable and might make selfish allies because they're immune to our magic?"

"So what animal do you want?"

"The alligators," Maga said without hesitation.

"Why?"

"Because I want to. I know they'd be best for me. I'm sure it will work out."

Grandma was silent, her hands still in her lap, the strange green knitting resting in her skirt. "They aren't immune to our magic," she finally said.

"But…you always said they were."

"There are some things they are immune to," the old woman conceded, "but our magic can do much more than you've seen yet."

"I've been studying with you forever!"

"And there were certain things you weren't allowed to see or do."

"And now?"

"Once you've got your eye, we'll work on the magic."

"Then what do I need to do next?"

Maga had always wondered at the work they did. Grandma seemed to be able to do so much more than Maga could. Witchery had to be more than plants and willpower. Her pulse thrummed at the thought.

"You need to find your donor."

"How do I do that?"

A thump on the door interrupted Grandma's answer. The two stared at each other before Grandma jerked her head in the direction of the door. Maga edged towards it before opening it carefully. Sitting in the doorway was everything she'd left at the tree including the blanket she'd left hanging over the branch. Standing behind the pile, a gleam in its golden eye, was the grizzled alligator, struggling to fit on the porch.

"I think you've found him" Grandma said from behind her, causing Maga to start. She hadn't heard the woman get up.

"But you've only got one working eye left," Maga protested, speaking to the gator before her.

He rumbled.

"Surely not. A blind alligator? Who's ever heard of such a thing?" Maga admonished him. "I couldn't do that to you."

Grandma put a hand on her shoulder. "He's volunteered. You have to honor that."

Maga shrugged the old woman's hand off her shoulder angrily. "No, I don't. It's suicide for him."

The gator growled, unhappy.

"I'm sorry, I just can't," Maga told him.

His tail swished back and forth, clearly agitated.

"Grandma, can you leave us, please?"

Maga didn't take her eyes off the leathery animal in front of her but felt the air shift and knew the old woman left. Stepping back into the doorway, Maga gestured for the gator to join her inside. He shuffled around the pile of stuff he'd left her, filling up the room. She was unable to shut the door but knew no one would dare eavesdrop on such a conversation.

"I really don't think this is a good idea," Maga told him again.

The alligator disagreed. He thought it was great idea. Did she want that young gator? He was a fool and would make a poor donor.

"At least he has an eye to spare," she retorted.

That didn't matter. He had more power to give her. She needed his eye.

"Well, you can't make me take it."

He snuffled and turned in the room. She watched him, wondering if he was about to leave. She hoped not, unsure if there was any other potential donor among the alligators. Maybe he was the only one willing. But he didn't leave. He dove into the pile, nosing around.

She heard the clink of glass and when he turned, rolling a jar, she saw something rolling around inside. Kneeling to pick it up, Maga almost dropped it when she saw what it was.

"Is this your eye?" she whispered, horrified.

See, she couldn't deny him now. He'd already had it removed.

The eye stared up at her from the jar and she swallowed. Suddenly everything felt very real and very imminent.

"I guess I can't say no," she agreed with a thick voice.

His answer was smug and she barely saw him leave, her gaze stuck on the yellow eye in the jar. Soon it would be her eye in the jar.

"Everything all sorted?" Grandma asked from the doorway.

"Uh huh," Maga said, distracted.

"Ready for that operation?"

"Now?" Maga squeaked, looking up at the old woman.

Grandma grinned. "We have some time before we need to do it but that eye won't last forever."

Maga swallowed again, hard and looked back down at the eye. She knew she wasn't going to change her mind. She might as well get it over with.

"Can Doxin be here for it?" she asked, barely recognizing her small, trembling voice.

"Of course. I'm going to need him to help hold you down."

Maga knew her face was frozen in a mask of horror. Grandma laughed and waved a hand at her.

"I'm teasing. I'll knock you out for some of it." Her face became serious once more. "But it's going to hurt."

Maga nodded.

"Are you sure about this?"

Maga nodded again.

"This is what you want?"

Maga held out the jar, the eye swiveling inside to stare at the swamp witch. She didn't need words and she wasn't sure she could form a single one. She knew Grandma would understand.

"Then let's get started."

The Swamp Witch

Grandma had been acting strangely for a few days now. Though her behavior could always be classed as strange, Maga had lived with the old woman for years and knew when it tipped over the limit of strange and into worrisome. But when Maga asked her, Grandma just muttered and turned away, refusing to answer.

"What do you think she's up to?" Maga asked Doxin when Grandma left her breakfast sitting on the wooden table, not even half-eaten.

Doxin looked up from his plate, his mouth bulging. His gaze flicked around the room and she could tell when he noticed Grandma was missing. Maga rolled her eyes.

"She not eating again?" Doxin replied after he swallowed his eggs.

"Yeah. What could possibly be going on with her?"

After her surgery, Maga found herself suddenly part of the witchery she always knew happened in the house but never really saw. Grandma treated her as a real apprentice, teaching her everything she needed to know about being a witch. But that didn't mean Grandma shared everything.

"Maybe I should ask again," Maga mused, pushing her own eggs around on her plate.

"Mmhmm," Doxin agreed, his eyes glazed over.

"Doxin!"

"What?" He looked up from his plate.

"Don't you think something strange is going on?"

Doxin swallowed his mouthful with a sigh. "You know she won't tell you if she doesn't want to. Pestering her isn't going to change that."

Maga glared at him, her golden eye narrowing. She knew he was right but his complete lack of concern over Grandma's bizarre behavior of late irritated her. Leaving her own eggs, she stormed out onto the porch. She could hear Grandma muttering in the workroom.

She didn't know how old the woman was, though Maga had lived with her for almost fifteen years. Was the woman getting too old? Senile, maybe? Maga couldn't tell and she wasn't about to ask.

Pushing the door open, Maga stared in at the odd tableau in front of her. Grandma was stretched up on her rocking chair, her toes grasping the arm rests as the chair rocked wildly against the cupboard. Her white hair standing out in a wispy halo, the old woman edged up the cupboard, obviously trying to reach something on top. Maga sprang forward, grabbing the arms of the rocking chair, stabilizing both the chair and the woman balanced on top.

Grandma looked down at her, smiling. "Thank you."

"What are you trying to get down? I can get it, if you like."

Maga was far more agile than Grandma would ever be. She spent most of her childhood climbing trees and skulking about the swamp.

"No need, girl, no need," Grandma tutted. Her hands stopped groping and she looked blankly down at Maga. "Do you need something?"

Stunned, Maga could only stutter a response. "No…I just came in and saw you…you were gonna fall. What are you looking for?"

"Oh, I wouldn't fall. Don't you worry about that. Don't you have some exercises to do?"

"Grandma, you stopped giving me exercises a year ago," Maga reminded the old woman.

"Hmm, so I did, so I did…"

Maga helped Grandma down from the rocking chair. As soon as the old woman was safely on the ground, Maga whisked the chair back to its place by the fire pit. She stared as Grandma wandered in circles, speaking to herself under her breath. The white-haired woman teetered around the room, rummaging through the containers littered about.

"What are you looking for?" Maga asked again, starting to get really worried.

"Nothing much, nothing much…"

Grandma finally found a piece of bark and some charcoal. She scribbled on it frantically, stood back to scrutinize it twice and then turned towards Maga, the bark in hand. She held it out, waving it until Maga finally approached, her alligator eye trying to discern if there was anything magical about the bark. She couldn't find anything and accepted it warily.

"I need these things," Grandma said. The foggy look was still in her eyes, her black, bird eye looking duller than Maga had ever seen it.

"What do you need them for?" Maga asked, not even looking down to see what she was supposed to fetch.

"Just need 'em," Grandma snapped, sounding more like her normal self again.

"Fine, ok, I'll go get them."

Doxin waited outside the door and Maga almost bumped into him.

"What's going on?" he asked, looking down at her from his superior height.

Maga glared as he loomed over her. She didn't like being reminded of their height difference and she could have sworn he did it on purpose. Stepping around him and off the porch, Maga headed for the shrubs and foliage that hid their clearing from the swamp around them.

"Grandma gave me a list of things she wants me to fetch," Maga told her familiar.

"What's on it?"

Maga held up the bark, trying to decipher Grandma's handwriting. "Swamp water, a flying head…I think this says nettles and I'm pretty sure this one is…metal?" Maga wasn't as sure she'd actually read that last one correctly.

Doxin took it from her hand, squinting at the bark. "The last one says metal bowl. I thought we had a metal bowl."

"Bowl?" Maga snatched it back. What she'd thought was a

scribble did actually look like the word bowl. "Damn, it does say bowl. You're right, I thought we had one of those…"

Handing the bark back to Doxin, Maga marched up the stairs leading to the porch. Grandma was crouched under the worktable and looked up guiltily when Maga opened the door.

"Grandma, what is going on here? You want a metal bowl? We already have one."

Grandma's face relaxed when she heard Maga and she crawled out from under the table, kicking something behind her, deeper into the shadows. Maga leaned to see what it was but Grandma was too quick and blocked her.

"Need a new metal bowl, girl."

"What happened to the old one?"

Grandma pointed to the fire pit. Maga stepped closer to see what the old woman was pointing at. Something shiny lay buried under the ashes. Maga crouched to sweep some of the ashes away with her hand. Their old metal bowl lay in a crumpled mess at the bottom of the fire pit.

Maga whirled to look at the old woman. "What on earth did you do to it?"

Grandma shrugged helplessly. "I don't know…it just sort of…melted."

"Of course it melted, look what you did to it! What were you doing?"

Grandma didn't answer, just looked her, the mismatched blue and black eye widened with confusion and feebleness. They stayed there, eyes locked on each other but the expression on Grandma's face didn't change. Maga sighed and stood up, brushing the ash from her hand onto her dirty skirt.

"So you need a new metal bowl?" Maga asked.

Grandma nodded, her face still stuck in the sort of expression that made her look like a normal old woman, one who couldn't bend trees, animals and people to her will. Maga didn't like the look of it. She stepped closer to the woman and laid a gentle hand on Grandma's quivering arm. The skin was like paper, thin and far too fragile.

"What's wrong, Grandma?" Maga asked the swamp witch.

"Nothing … I … the list!" Grandma grabbed Maga's arm, her nails digging into her skin.

"The piece of bark you just gave me?"

"The list!"

"It's ok, Grandma. Doxin has it. We'll go get you everything you need, ok?" Maga patted the old woman's hand as the grip relaxed. She tugged Grandma over to the rocking chair and sat her down in it.

On her way out, Maga glanced under the table where Grandma had been crouched. She didn't see anything through the yawning shadows but she didn't stop to look harder. It was obvious that Grandma needed those four items if just for her peace of mind.

"Ready to go?" Doxin asked when she reappeared on the porch.

"Yeah, let's go. Sooner we get those things and get back, hopefully the sooner she'll be back to her old self."

"Did you solve the mystery of the metal bowl?"

"She melted the old one," Maga told Doxin, rolling her eyes.

An easy flick of her eyes had the bushes rolling back from the two of them. After her surgery, which Maga winced to even think about, controlling the wildlife around the house was as simple as a thought. Like so many other things.

"How are you planning on getting a flying head?" Doxin asked, trailing her through the path she created.

"I haven't figured it out but I'm sure we'll come across one somewhere. The swamp's supposed to be full of them."

"Surely they aren't stupid enough to take a swipe at you…"

"I'm not a swamp witch yet, Doxin. Besides, it's you they'll avoid."

One of the things she learned about familiars is that they weren't exactly fragile. There were safety spells woven into their being that gave them an added measure of security, something they could often extend to others.

"True."

"I'm sure we'll find one."

"Then what about a metal bowl? Do you even know where she got that last one?"

"We'll just have to find a dump and hope there's a bowl there."

Doxin didn't ask any more questions to Maga's relief. She had enough of her own whirling around in her brain and they didn't all pertain to the strange list Grandma had given her.

"I think we'll do the nettles and water at the end," Maga said after the silence penetrated her thoughts.

"That's fine. Get the hard stuff first."

They walked in silence, Maga leading Doxin, though where, she wasn't sure. She knew there had to be a dump around somewhere. Though the three of them lived quite centrally in the swamp, and dumps tended to be gathered around the edges of the watery terrain, Grandma had enough stuff that couldn't have come from anywhere else.

"You got a plan?" Doxin asked when it became obvious she wasn't leading so much as wandering.

"Not really. Just hoping to find someone who might know where one is."

"Hmm." Doxin didn't mention that no one lived especially close by. They rarely saw other people. But she didn't need him to tell her that. "Do you think she sent us on a wild goose chase?" he asked after another minute of silence.

"The thought crossed my mind."

"Then why are we out here?"

"I don't think she'd ask us to bring her a head unless she needed it. We aren't trained to protect ourselves from them."

'But we can,' Doxin told her. "Protect ourselves, that is."

"Of course," she replied.

But when the time came for them to protect themselves, neither of them were ready.

Maga heard the flying heads long before she saw them. They both pulled their knives, the only weapons they carried and readied themselves. By the sound of the heads, the clacking of their teeth and the nerve-wrenching chittering sound, there was definitely more than one of them.

With her golden gator eye, Maga didn't have to worry about the mesmerizing gaze of the heads. Grandma assured them that Doxin wouldn't have to worry about it either. As a familiar, he was protected from that somehow.

So when she finally saw two of them, Maga wasn't afraid to face them, her knife ready before her. She felt Doxin shift behind her and she knew he must have spotted them as well. The heads circled them, screeching, swooping past them but staying far enough away from the sharp ends of the knives. She could see the stars in their eyes, little sparkling flecks, the essence of the monsters.

Maga's blood thrummed with adrenaline. She wasn't sure if they'd be stupid enough to attack. Heads weren't renowned for their intelligence and she didn't know if they recognized her as anything other than a simple human.

"Maga," Doxin said nervously from behind her. "Can't you do something?" Neither of them had any experience with the protection he possessed and they weren't sure how it worked or how far it went.

She could do something but she wanted to see what the heads came for. It didn't seem as simple as a hunt. They hovered over herself and Doxin, occasionally swooping but mostly, it seemed, just looking. However, Maga could hear the tension in her familiar's voice and feel it in his muscles. She'd have to end it before he did something rash.

A flick of her wrist pulled the climbing thorns down from a nearby tree, ripping them from the grasp they had on the bark. Another quick gesture directed them towards the nearest head and then she let go, letting gravity do the rest of the work. The head screamed as the net of thorns fell, pinning it in the swampy marsh below. The other three heads circled, crying in reply, confusion causing them to spin and dip crazily as they flew through the air.

Doxin yelled and charged at one of them, wielding his knife in a large, capable hand. Maga tried not the watch, wanting to make certain that the head caught in the thorns was really captured. It didn't take long for her familiar to chase the others away, his own flickering abilities lending him aid as energy jolts followed the remaining heads' every move until they disappeared from sight entirely.

He came to a stop beside her, panting, as she stared down at the head. It stopped moving but keened, the high pitched sound running right through her and rattling her teeth.

"What are we going to do with it?" Doxin asked.

"Take it back to Grandma."

Between the two of them, and Maga's ability with the plants, they wrapped the head up safely. A length of the vine, stripped of its thorns, made a nice handle and though Doxin was wary at first, he accepted the burden. The head swung between them as they walked, still making noises.

"Do they ever shut up?" Doxin asked when he couldn't stand

it any longer.

"Grandma says they don't."

"Anyone within a mile radius of us will know we're here," he grumbled.

"Do you just want to take it back now? Go get the other stuff after?"

"No, it's fine. I just want to get all this over with."

As they walked, Maga tried to think of how to find a dump quicker than just wandering around. An idea jumped out at her from her jumble of thoughts and she came to an abrupt stop. Doxin walked on a few steps further before he realized.

"What is it?" he asked.

"I know how we'll find a dump faster."

Maga didn't hear if he asked how she planned on doing that. She was already busy. While the outside world was silent, aside from the soft sounds of anxiety the head emitted, her head buzzed with the internal noise of thought. She reached through her own mess of chaos and into the one that only ever seemed two steps away.

She never could have predicted the ways her surgery would affect her. Grandma said it touched everyone differently and because the eye wasn't from a familiar, there was really no telling what might happen. What happened was that her donor, a crafty, older alligator was never far from her thoughts. With only a small prod, she felt his internal eye turn her way.

Standing stock still, Maga waited. She didn't need words to tell the gator what she was looking for or how she wanted his help. He took the pictures she showed and then his focus shifted away. Maga pulled back into her own mind, brushing past the other sphere never far from her own.

Doxin turned and took a step closer. She felt his mental sphere grow bigger and brush lightly against hers. Tightening her sphere, she kept quiet. The alligator would help her solve this dilemma swiftly. She didn't want to waste time hunting for a dump to find a metal bowl. Who knew what Grandma was up to in their absence?

Neither of them said anything for minutes. She felt Doxin's patience nearing an end as the head in his hand keened and shook within the thorn cage she created for it. Maga hoped Grandma didn't want her to kill it once they got home. Despite its ghastly appearance and appetite for human flesh, Maga wasn't a killer.

"Maga, look." Doxin pointed with his free hand.

In the distance, light winked off of a strange object. They lost it behind plants and trees but it bobbed ever closer. A metal bowl materialized from behind a screen of foliage, carried along in the water by a familiar face.

Maga bellowed a greeting as the one-eyed alligator slunk into view. It rumbled a reply, the bowl on its head quivering. She flashed a smile at Doxin before splashing through the water to greet her friend. Since the operation, Maga became much closer to the alligators. She hadn't realized it beforehand but donating an eye to a swamp witch came with honors and stature. The alligator elevated his status through her but she didn't mind. Such a willing volunteer had been welcome.

They traded a few pleasantries but the alligator knew she was eager to be off. With a growl of thanks, Maga spun and dove into the swamp, heading for home. She'd pick up some nettles on the way. Doxin, surprised by the quickness of her visit with the gator, was caught out behind her. He had to rush to catch up but she knew he wouldn't get lost.

"I thought we'd have to go to the dump ourselves," Doxin panted as he ducked under a low branch, lengthening his stride to stay abreast of her.

"He knew it was kind of urgent but I didn't expect him to bring one either. He said there was one lying around."

"Really? Alligators have stuff like that just lying around?" Doxin's skepticism was barely reigned in at all.

Maga flicked him an amused look. Sometimes he had funny reactions to the alligators. She thought he maybe resented the help they gave her or the time she spent with them. He certainly wasn't pleased about the depth of her connection to her donor.

While Maga knew Doxin was grateful she'd never asked him to give her one of his blue eyes, she thought he regretted the connection they lacked because of it. Familiars and their witches always shared an eye, but then, familiars had always been animals before. At seventeen she hadn't been able to make herself ask him for an eye. And she didn't think she'd have been able to accept it if he'd offered.

"You didn't answer my question," Doxin said.

"I didn't realize it was a question."

"Doesn't he have anything better to do? Couldn't he have just given you directions?"

"Did you really want to go to the dump that badly? Maybe I can ask him for directions tomorrow."

"That's not what I was saying and you know it."

"Doxin, can you withhold your suspicions for ten minutes. There're bigger things going on than that."

"I know, I know, I'm just pointing it out."

"I know you are," Maga replied. "And I appreciate you looking out for us."

Doxin looked slightly mollified at that and even showed her a patch of nettles she hadn't seen. Carefully wrapping a length of fabric around her hand, Maga picked three stalks. She had her hands full but they weren't far from home and she didn't expect an attack. Heads stayed away from the clearing and the witches, for the most part. Their behavior today was inexplicable but it was a worry for another day. She dipped the bowl on her way, gathering swamp water in its bottom. She didn't want to forget anything.

When Maga finally peeled back the foliage surrounding the clearing, creating a path for both of them and their supplies, she was startled to hear banging and curses emanating from the workroom. Maga looked over at Doxin, worried. His expression mirrored hers and they hurried, leaping up onto the porch. Doxin thrust the door open.

"Grandma?" Maga couldn't see the witch, though the workroom was a disaster. "Are you ok?"

Maga sidled into the room warily. She knew it couldn't be anyone other than her mentor, they had enough wards laid down that she would have known if someone broke in. Laying her burdens down on the work table, she called for the old woman once more. The room wasn't large enough to hide an adult but Maga knew she'd heard the sounds from in here somewhere.

Doxin stood by the door and when Maga turned to look at him, he shrugged. The head hanging from his hand wailed louder, as if aware its time was nearly over. Maga shrieked and jumped backwards as Grandma's head popped out from under the table.

Glaring, and trying to recover her composure, Maga panted. Grandma ignored her and climbed out from under the table, heading straight for Doxin and his burden. She took the head from Doxin, holding it up to her face. The head shrunk back as far as the thorns would allow it, its noises dying away almost entirely.

"Hmm…good, good," Grandma muttered.

Maga stood back as the old woman marched back over to the table. The witch finally noticed the swamp water in the metal bowl and the nettles lying next to it. She nodded, looking pleased and she swung the head up onto the table. It screamed as the thorns pierced its thick skin. Grandma tutted and with a knife, sawed at the twisting vines.

Maga stepped back involuntarily as the head sprung free. It hovered, confused, as if it didn't know where to go. But before it could make a move, Grandma flung a hand up. A flash of light illuminated the room and when Maga's eyes cleared, the head hung in a dim ball of light, immobilized. She saw it open its mouth wider to screech but the sound never left its prison.

Grandma lost interest in the head immediately, turning to the bowl. She poured the swamp water over the table and stomped the nettles beneath her feet.

"Hey!" Doxin stepped forward, his brows puckered angrily.

Maga held up a hand, stopping him but it was too late, Grandma remembered their presence. Turning to look at them, Grandma stared with confusion.

"You can go," the old woman said, waving dismissively.

"Are you sure you wouldn't like some help?" Maga asked. She didn't know what the woman was doing but she wanted to stay and watch.

"No, no, you'll only get in the way."

Maga knew better than to argue with the witch. Doxin seemed less willing to leave without a firmer declaration from Grandma but when Maga tugged him away from the room, he followed without a word.

Next door, in the communal room, Maga paced as she tried to figure out what Grandma wanted with the list she'd sent them on a hunt for. Doxin thought he already knew.

"She just wanted us out of the room, Maga."

"But a head? Why would she send us after a head for fun?"

"Well, maybe she needed that," he conceded, "but the other stuff? All she had to do was step off the porch for some swamp water and nettles are a dime a dozen around here."

Maga couldn't disagree. "But what could she want the head for and how did she melt the other bowl?"

"Maybe she's getting too old," Doxin suggested.

"Maybe."

Maga didn't want to think about it but Grandma's behavior of late did seem like symptoms of old age. Even though Maga had lived with the old woman for so many years, Grandma never seemed to get older, she just stayed the same. Maga couldn't imagine a life without her but the woman had to be ancient by now.

"Why don't you go check on her, see what she's doing?"

Maga frowned as she paced. "I don't know; what if she isn't going senile? What if she's actually doing something important?"

Doxin shrugged. Maga huffed. "Fine. I'll be back, don't move."

Mag crept out of the communal room and onto the porch. The sounds from the workroom were subdued but she could hear Grandma muttering to herself. It was a new habit Maga didn't like. It made the old woman seem frail.

The window shutter was open and Maga peeked over the sill, trying to make out the shapes and shadows within the dim room. Grandma had the metal bowl over the fire, the head immobilized in its ball of light not far above. The old woman looked away from the bowl, glaring up at the head. Maga saw the head's mouth moving but nothing came out.

"I heard you," Grandma growled at the head.

Maga's eyes widened and she leaned closer, trying to see if she could hear anything.

"That's not good enough, I need to know more."

Grandma hadn't sounded so coherent in weeks. Maga couldn't decide if it had all been a façade for her benefit or not. There wasn't a reason she could think of that Grandma would hide something that sounded so important from her. While Maga wasn't a full swamp witch, she was the old woman's apprentice and she needed to know a lot more than Grandma chose to share. Like the spell that had the head suspended in midair. Maga had never seen that before.

A squawk snapped Maga out of her thoughts and her alligator eye caught on the black eye of Grandma's familiar. With a gasp, Maga ducked, plastering herself to the side of the house. She knew she was spotted and the flutter of wings overhead told her she wouldn't get away that easily.

She looked up sheepishly into the single eye of the downy

woodpecker. He cocked his head at her, staring down at her from his perch on the window sill.

"Ok, ok, I'm going," Maga grumbled as she crawled to her feet. With a nasty look over her shoulder, she left the workroom and the mystery it held behind her.

"Well?" Doxin asked when she reappeared in the doorway. He sat at the table, his mouth full of whatever he had on his plate.

She flopped down on the bench across from him. "I don't know what's going on but I don't think she's losing her mind."

"That's good news, right?"

"Yeah, I guess so." But that only opened the door to more questions.

When they went their separate ways for the night, Maga couldn't fall asleep. Her mind buzzed with the unanswered questions. There were still noises coming from the workroom when her mind finally shut down and allowed her some peace and sleep. It was silence that woke her.

Sitting up in bed, Maga looked around her, trying to pinpoint what was out of place. She finally realized it was the quiet and she jumped out of bed, scurrying down the porch to the workroom. Pressing her ear to the door, Maga didn't hear anything inside.

She pushed open the door, her golden eye immediately cataloguing its neatness. Yesterday when she and Doxin arrived back, the workroom had been a mess. It was obvious that Grandma had been looking for something in their absence. Everything had been pulled out of place and littered around the room. In contrast, the room before her now was spotless. Every single item was put back in order, the closet closed, the blanket folded, and the remnants of the spell she saw last night, entirely cleared away.

A sound at her feet made her bite back a cry. She hadn't even noticed the gator approaching though she felt its rough, dry skin brush against her calf. He looked up at her, amusement gleaming in his one eye.

"What are you doing here?" Maga hissed.

His quiet rumble told her that something was going on with Grandma, and with the swamp.

"Do you know what it is?"

He shook his head, his mind a jumble of thoughts she couldn't quite reach. A sudden sound inside, beyond the work room, snapped their attention around.

Grandma emerged from the door to her room, in her hands balanced the metal bowl, brimming with some murky liquid. The head bobbed along behind her, still stuck in its spherical prison. Its mouth still moved, and to Maga it looked angry and worried.

"Oh, hi, girl," Grandma said when she finally looked up and noticed Maga standing there, the alligator by her feet.

"What are you doing?" Maga asked.

Grandma shuffled past them to lay the bowl on the work table. "I think you should send your little friend away. We need to have a chat."

Maga looked down at the gator. He did the equivalent of a shrug and turned, swiping both her and Grandma with his tail, before shuffling out through the doorway. She felt his mind pull further and further away.

"Well?" Maga asked, crossing her arms over her chest.

"I'm leaving."

It took a moment for the words to register in Maga's mind. When they finally did, she could feel her jaw sag.

"What?"

Grandma pushed some of her white hairs out of her face. She nudged the stool over to Maga who sat.

"I'm leaving," the old woman repeated.

Maga didn't even know which question to ask first.

"You're going to be the swamp witch now."

Maga's head snapped up. "What do you mean?"

"I'm leaving. I already said that. But the swamp still needs a witch."

"Why are you going? I'm not ready to be the swamp witch. I barely know anything." For all the spells and abilities she had, Maga knew there was so much more Grandma kept from her.

"I need to go. There's something happening."

"What thing? Why can't you fix it here?"

"I don't know everything I need to."

"Well, neither do I! I don't know anything about being the swamp witch. You don't teach me anything!" As soon as she said it, Maga knew that was unfair. Grandma spent years teaching her but she just didn't feel like it was enough. She didn't feel prepared to be the swamp witch, for Grandma to leave her.

"There's only so much I can teach you," Grandma told her. "The rest of it you'll need to figure out on your own. Like your relationships."

Maga gaped at the old woman.

"Don't look at me like that. We're different kind of witches and I've done what I can. It'll be better when I'm not here."

With that, Grandma picked up her bowl and headed for the door. It took Maga a moment to realize that was everything Grandma had to say. Springing to her feet, Maga raced after the old woman, who moved quicker than she should have been able to. When Maga made it to the doorway herself, the bushes and trees that protected the clearing were parting for Grandma.

"Wait!" Maga called after her, rushing down off the porch.

But when she made it to the edge, the bushes snapped back together. Maga couldn't pull them a part and she heard her mentor get further and further away.

"Maga?" Doxin appeared on the porch looking worried. "Maga, what's wrong?"

"She left," Maga replied numbly.

"Grandma?"

Maga nodded, slowly heading back to the house that was all hers and Doxin's now. Doxin came to meet her, grabbing her arms and looking down into her face.

"Where'd she go? When's she coming back?"

"I don't know. She isn't coming back."

"What do you mean she isn't coming back?" Doxin sounded as worried as she was when she first heard Grandma tell her.

"I'm the swamp witch now."

EXCERPT: A SWAMP OF BONES

CHAPTER 1

Makani stood ankle-deep in the muck. There was dirt under her
blindfold and it itched but she refused to take a hand off her stave to
scratch. She shifted her stance, her ears straining and sifting through
the sounds of the swamp.

The small noises of the foragers behind her were always the
same. The tearing of vegetation, the small grunts of effort, the slosh
of their feet moving through the swamp. Even the other guard had
his own sounds. She'd been paired with Russ this time. Makani didn't
know much about him aside from his name and the fact that this was
only his third outing as a guard.

Sometimes these forays into the swamp were more than boring.
The foragers in this camp, where she'd only been a few months, were
not as well trained as they were in other camps. These foragers were
younger than most and weren't very efficient. Makani knew she could
do a better job but her skills as a guard were more in demand.

"Maki…Is this safe?" Isaac asked. She knew he was holding
something up and she restrained a sigh.

"Bring it over here," she told him. Unlike so many others in the
swamp, Makani refused to remove her blindfold. She didn't want to
take the risk.

Isaac sloshed through the swamp waters that separated them. He
thrust a bundle of leaves into her face. Makani reared back, grabbing
his hand. Steadying it, she dipped her nose into the leaves. She let go
of his hand to stroke her fingers through the offering to try and make

out what it was. It felt like wild carrot or Queen Anne's lace but she knew it wasn't.

Makani snatched it from him. "Smell it," she said, shoving it towards his face. Isaac took a deep breath in through his nose. "Does it smell like a carrot? Is it furry?"

She could feel the air currents change as he shook his head. "It's fool's parsley," Makani told him, throwing it on the ground and stomping on it with one thick soled boot. "Poison. Don't pick it again, ok?"

"Ok," Isaac said, shaken. He backed away, the leather bag at his side thumping against his body as he moved.

Someday she knew one of the foragers would bring something poisonous back to the camp mistakenly. It was only a matter of time.

Makani turned her back on the small band, facing outwards once again. With only two guards it was hard to create a ring of protection around the kids but she tried her best.

"What was that?" Russ whispered, his voice carrying.

Makani froze. She hadn't heard anything out of the ordinary. She could smell the sharp stench of Russ' sweat but didn't hear whatever he'd heard.

"I thought-" Russ said, cutting himself off.

Makani strained. She still didn't hear anything and the enemy was always loud. They never failed to announce themselves.

"I don't hear anything," Makani told him.

He ignored her. "Come on, kids, hurry up," Russ said loudly. She could hear that he was trying to be commanding but it came out whiney and scared.

The foragers, infected with his nerves, hurried. She heard one of them trip and fall, splashing into the swamp waters. Someone started crying. Makani tried to keep her impatience to herself. Russ was just making things worse for no reason.

"Ok, let's go," Russ said. Makani knew he didn't have his blindfold on. He hustled the three kids onwards, back towards the camp and she turned to follow them. It was her job.

Over the sounds of them splashing through the swamp, fear making them go faster and faster, Makani heard it. The sound they'd been listening for.

"They're here," she shouted. "Kids, to me!"

Someone screamed, she thought it was Isaac but it might have been Eliza. The chatter of the incoming zombies was impossible to miss. She wasn't sure if it was their teeth or their laughter but something grated on something, creating that dreadful noise. Three sets of hands were suddenly on her, Russ shouting something over the chaos of sounds.

"Blindfolds!" Makani shouted over him. He was old enough to live and die by his own stupidity. The kids weren't.

She tried to count the number of zombies in the swarm, tried to keep her mind calm through the chaos around her. The noises were still seconds away, giving her time to count, time to plan. She couldn't move in any direction, the crowd of children at her feet chaining her to the spot. But she didn't need to move.

Makani kept the stave in her hand sharpened. The wicked blade at the end of it kept her alive though it had taken years of training with it. Russ stumbled away from them, shouting obscenities. He was unintentionally leading the swarm away from her and the kids.

"Run," Makani said, changing the plan. Russ was getting further and further away and the camp wasn't too far. They could make it.

Isaac whimpered and Makani reached down, grabbing him by his thin shirt. She hauled him up, pushing him in the direction of the camp. "Run!" she said again, nudging the other children with the toe of her boot. It took them a moment but they got up and starting running as fast as they could through the swamp.

Makani heard Russ flailing about far off to her left. His shouting had died down and she knew he was fighting off five of them. It sounded as if he'd managed to get his blindfold up or he wouldn't have lasted this long. Torn between going to his side and running after the kids to make sure they got back safely, the decision was made for her. As his screams strangled in his throat, dying, Makani knew it was too late to help him.

Pivoting on one foot, she launched herself after the kids. Who knew if there was another swarm about. One of the flying zombie heads detached itself from the swarm behind her. She heard it chittering as it flew after her. Makani kept running, hoping it would give up and return to the rest of its kind. It didn't.

With a growl she spun around, jabbing with her stave. The heads weren't very smart and they died easily. The blade at the end of her staff ripped up through the bottom of its face and the chittering abruptly stopped. It fell from the air to land with a plop in the swamp.

Makani heard something behind her and she whipped around, her stave up in a defensive position.

"It's just me," Isaac said, his voice shaking.

She heaved a sigh and planted the stave in the muddy earth below. Taking a step back, she felt a crunch under her boot. Another bone.

"I've never seen one like this before," Isaac said, stepping closer. They weren't far from the camp but far enough she knew she should scold him for being out in the open.

He squatted in the swamp where she'd heard the head fall. Dead, they were no danger to anyone. No one really knew much about them except that to look into their eyeless sockets was death.

"There aren't any wings or anything," Isaac said, wonder in his voice. "And no eyes. None at all. It's like… It's like they were ripped out or something."

Makani huffed. "Isaac, let's go inside."

He sighed but stood up, kicking at the head. "Where's Russ?" Isaac asked as he followed her back towards the camp.

"He died," she told him shortly.

Death was nothing new in the swamp. Children grew up knowing all about it. Makani's father died when she was eight and the rest of her family scattered. She had no way of knowing if any of them were still alive though she ranged from camp to camp in the swamp, searching for answers.

"Oh. I think I liked him."

Makani didn't know what to say in response to that. She just kept walking, Isaac trudging along behind her. The entrance to the camp was hard to find for anyone who didn't know what they were looking for.

There weren't solid structures in the swamp. The camps were based on islands of dry land, surrounded by bushes and thorns to keep the people inside hidden and somewhat safe. Isaac crawled through the small entrance and Makani followed, relieved to be back. All three foragers made it home alive so she considered the outing a success.

Unfortunately, they'd need another guard to replace Russ. Makani knew whoever they picked would be even less qualified than Russ had been. She didn't relish this part of camp living; watching ill-prepared people forced into roles they would die at. She could feel an itch in her shoulder blades that said it was getting time to move on.

AFTERWORD

Thanks for reading!

ALSO BY THE AUTHOR:

BORN SERIES
Born in the Mouth of an Angel
Born on the Run
Born from the Ashes
Born for a Better Life

THE SWAMP CHILDREN
Novels
A Swamp of Bones
A Swamp of Souls
A Swamp of Lies
Things in the Swamp
The Swamp Witches

ANTHOLOGIES
Searching for Finding
Patience, Violence & Other Stories of Change
When our Amulets Fail us

NOVELETTES
The Locket
The Amaranthine Dowager
The Poisoned Perfume

SHORT STORIES
Just Another Shop
Just Another Customer
The Problem of Carl and Louie
Patience, Violence and the Red, Red Moon
The Twisted Tree
Tricks, Games & Insanity
Leipreachán
The Gothic Ghost Killer

ABOUT THE AUTHOR

Abigail Fero is an American fantasy writer whose work is bound by a love of the unreal and the impossible. She hopes that you'll find something to enjoy in her body of work. You can find her books online and find out more about her on her website: abigailfero.blogspot.com